I0755896

MORE POEMS AND OTHER FAIRY TALES 2021–2026

MORE POEMS

and OTHER FAIRY TALES

1921–2026

Fairy Tales Charley Boving

Kees Nydam KN

Can you keep a secret? In 1962, I was 8 turning 9 and Malvina Reynolds penned a chart busting satirical song called 'Little Boxes'. She wrote about pretty children going to summer camp and then on to university. Some would become lawyers, and of these lawyers, some would go into copyright law. In turn these folk would generate ISBNs to put into boxes, like the one below. In a parallel universe, exists a narrative of song-catchers who channel the songs of the village community, each a 'medium' who captures what is already there. Thus, ownership of these songs belongs to the whole. The same could be said about poetry. Using a basic mental model, stealing from one is plagiarism, thieving from thousands is research. Mark Twain, recognising this conundrum, said "Only one thing is impossible for God: To find any sense in any copyright law on the planet." My secret is that my inner 8 or 9 year-old child thinks that copyright law, is very *ticky-tacky*. Only those familiar with the song will get the reference! Awkward then, that in order to nurture our inner children, the grown-ups in the global village need to earn a crust. D'oh!

I am comforted though that no one reads anything written on the copyright page. So, this secret is safe. At least I hope so.

First Published in 2026 by Echo Books

Echo Books is an imprint of Superscript Publishing Pty Ltd
ABN 76 644 812 395
35 Keeley Lane, Princes Hill, Victoria, 3054
www.echobooks.com.au

ISBN: 978-1-923441-96-5

PROLOGUE

I broke in my mid-forties with many things contributing to my meltdown. Like Humpty Dumpty, I had a great fall. Unlike Humpty, Dumpty I could and was put back together again; welded with gold. The gold in my case was to be found in poetry and songwriting, pursuits that I had developed in my teens but had allowed to whither on the vine. This may have been called journalling to some, but to me it was writing to uncover my truths in a cosmos where truth was ultimately unknowable. It was a way of reflecting on the many absurdities, ironies and paradoxes that flashed before me daily. Chronicling the nonsense of it all helped me carry on.

Sartre, the French philosopher said "before you come alive, life is nothing; it's up to you to give it a meaning, and the value is nothing else but the meaning that you choose". *Poems and Other Fairy Tales* are my diary of meanings.

I was never really broken. I just needed to enter a new and more magnanimous space. I learnt that one of our paramount strengths as humans is our vulnerability. Perfectionism is an illusion that traps many. Another strength is our openness to receive greater bandwidth. Paradox and irony are axiomatic to our being. My poems aims to explore those axioms.

I hope they might mean something for you.

Kees

CONTENTS

ART, MUSIC AND MOVEMENT

AUSTRALIANNA

HISTORY AND THE CLASSICS

TRAVEL AND EXPLORATION

LOVE AND INTIMACY

GRATITUDE

INNER CHILD AND OTHER FAIRY TALES

SCIENCE, SICK-OLOGY & MEDICINE

MORALITY, STRUGGLE, GOD AND CONFLICT

MORTALITY AND IMMORTALITY

MY CHILDREN

ART, MUSIC and MOVEMENT

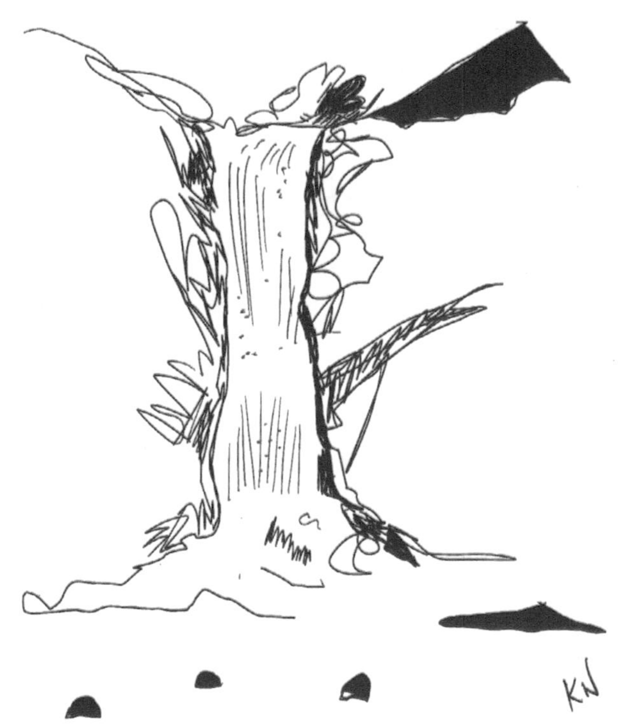

Kakadu Waterfall

"Art holds a pivotal position in the framework of human civilisation, acting as a medium to convey emotions, share ideas, and forge connections that go beyond the limitations of time and geography." – Professor Sarah Wilson, art historian and curator, at Courtauld Institute of Art, UK.

ART and CRAFT

art and craft
are antidotes
to mankind's folly
they're our lifeboats

they create
anecdotes
reminding us
of who and why we are

they may differ
in form and function
still they're
our guiding star

there's theatre
music, painting
sculpture and dance
amid other modes

the finest art
is original
yet, don't forget creators
steal like artists

artists say
they caught something
already there
wafting in the air

the artist
is just the conduit
needed to reveal it
I fully get it

art and craft
are antidotes
to mankind's folly
they're our lifeboats

"The world today doesn't make sense, so why should I paint pictures that do?" – Pablo Picasso

Nielsons Park Beach, Bargara March 2025

I've long felt an affinity with Kurt Vonnegut. When I came across a letter he wrote in 2006, it so gripped me, that I felt I had to replicate Kurt's theme in a poem.

ART IS A BALLOON

dear Xavier
thanks for your letter
you sure know how to
cheer up an old geezer

what I wanna say
won't take long, to wit
practice any art at all
even if you suck at it

not for the money
nor the fame
merely to feel
the euphoria you gain

that sweet spot
inside of you
that soothes
your soul

singing dancing
drawing painting
doesn't matter what you do
as long as it
uplifts you

start right now
dance rather than walk
draw a smiley face
on a dirty window

pretend to be
Count Dracula
sing your heart out
in the shower

acting dancing
sculpting drawing
doesn't matter what you do
as long as it uplifts you

as soon
as you start
you'll already
be rewarded

your soul
will grow
moving you forward
your spirit will fly
in a dazzling sky

Inspired and adapted from Kurt Vonnegut's 2006 *Amazing Letter To A High School*

Sharon May 2024

I was contemplating the phrase "kill your darlings", a phrase attributed to many deep thinkers. In my writing, I hurl words onto a page in a frenzy, then spend days editing in a ruthless slash and burn manoeuvre i.e. "killing darlings". These days ofttimes my wife joins in the massacre.

BINGE-GUT-N-PITCH

So, you wanna be a poet, then sit at your Mac
binge and bleed onto the screen
Let your fantasies be air balloons that raise you up
to a plane way beyond the rational
You want to be a writer, then sit
and write like the Dickens

Have your pen pour your mind's crazy onto the page
onto the tabletop, even spill onto the floor
Let your creative juice rain like a monsoon that swamps all
then have an editor tidy up your frenzied artistry

Allow the foetus of your vision, to bud and bloom
beyond the womb of your intellect, then splash
its life-waters atop the gumboots of the editor-midwife

So, you want to be a wordsmith, then don't mourn
when with a surgeon's precision they gut
more than you desired

Remember that the reader wants it lean
give them ample airspace for their imagination
to pad and fill the gaps

Wanna write then write for them, respect their sovereignty
coz that's the source of their joy
Sit at your desk and bleed; then get another to mop up the spills
like a mother, you're only part of the process
your job's not done till you ditch and let go

"Writing is like carrying a foetus." – Edna O'Brien (b. 15 Dec 1930)

Bargara Dec 2021, revised Oct 2024

I encountered the word *denouement* in early secondary school. I thought it was so cool to have a single French word mean the same as the entire sentence "the final resolution of the intricacies of a plot, as of a drama or novel" in English. Curiously a final resolution of anything signals the end. Why would we want an end, when being caught up in the plot is so much fun. Surely we should call for a stay of execution. A denouement ironically calls for a eulogy. Language has over 50 shades of grey.

DENOUEMENT

I suck at making calls, cuz nothing's all or nothing
verdicts're never tight, there's always a sequel
forever something sandwiched in-between
no ruling's perfect, that's my for real deal

We all want the gold cache, stashed at the rainbow's end
I say enjoy what you have, cold-shoulder what you want
take care for yearnings pay a poor dividend
life's still amazing, be grateful you're still breathing

You're lucky when you're neighbourless
they often love to raise awareness, they prey
concrete's ne'er factual, abstract's more actual
there's so many choices, when everything is grey

Nothing's as it seems; we see what we wanna
we all wanna taste the honey pot
we all want to stoke our own bias
just try being nice; you might hit the jackpot

I suck at making calls, cuz nothing's all or nothing
there's always something buried in-between
luckily I know, I can pass the baton on
give someone else a chance, to call the denouement

My neighbours, they take me as I am
we don't trade on favours, or do chameleon
I watch them pass me by, I'm glad I'm not their prey
for us, there's no denouement, we all want to stay
the final curtain, keep the last act uncertain

Bargara Feb 2024

The death poem is a style of poetry that offers a reflection on death, both in general and concerning the imminent death of the author. It is often coupled with a meaningful observation on life. It was initially composed in the Haiku form, in order to be expressed in one breath. The practice of writing a death poem has its origins in Zen Buddhism. Buddhism arrived in Japan in the 6th century and merged with Shinto, the native belief system. The Buddhist worldview contains three marks of existence:

1. The material world is transient and impermanent.
2. Attachment to the material word causes suffering.
3. Ultimately all reality is an emptiness of self-nature.

Death poems were customarily composed by Japanese samurai (prior to battle), noblemen, monks, and poets. As a wannabe poet, I felt obliged to give Haiku a go, using a Marcus Aurelius quote for inspiration (see below).

My current view of existence is that we are all mere molecules, dislodged from a universe of molecules for a nanosecond before we rejoin the universe again.

HAIKU X 2

I flew into this
'twas a place I'd never been
I landed sight unseen

A vision appeared
it took my breath away
the next will be even better

Inspiration – "Think of yourself as dead. You have lived your life.
Now take what's left and live it properly." – Marcus Aurelius

Bargara Jan 2025

I do it all the time. Do you? I see a taxi driver and from the rear seat am only able to view him rear side on. He has unkempt hair and 1900's muttonchop sideburns. My mind immediately constructs a narrative of that person. I am totally aware that the narrative is based on flimsy evidence. It's a game. Sometimes, we may connect and I will discover just how off track I was. It reminds me that I don't have to practice to be wrong.

IPSWICH MAN

Initial scan
reads Ipswich man
based on vision
of half a face

Down the road
a quarter mile
his mp3 shuffle
made me smile

The song I heard
was a track-o-mine
the soundtrack anchored
us in time

Hasty hunches
strung along
don't need to practice
to be wrong

Never had to practice
to be wrong

A sole USB
airs his past
born in Brazil, he said
when I asked

First cup of tea – a stranger
next cup of tea – a chum
third cup of tea – a brother
in a house for all & everyone

My eyes are drawn to
a girl 'cross the street
I caught a vision
only half a face

M' brain ran out
a makeshift yarn
sure bet that tale
will be wrong again

Never had to practice
being wrong

Reference: *Three Cups Of Tea* by Greg Mortenson

Brisbane Jan 2020

Is That All There Is became a hit for the American singer Peggy Lee in 1969. It was a favourites of my mum. The lyrics are written from the perspective of a person who is always disappointed with life events. Possibly an over-thinker. But I do like her retort to her disappointment: *If that's all there is my friends, then let's keep dancing, let's break out the booze and have a ball.* This is my homage to that song.

IS WHAT IT IS

Follow me into the breach
ain't no high we can't reach
do a *grand jeté* like an uber-bitch
with a battery pack sewn beneath her skin
giving her oomph, an energy that's more
than just skin-deep, we'd all like
to be like her
a crazed spirit nymph

We're all, each other, all alike
nine billion one-man skiffle bands
bodies gyrating to music
minds ploughed headlong into sand
knowing the going's tough
when is enough, enough
not now; talk to the hand
we're all dancing in a mindless trance

Let's all have a ball
treat life as a dance
your mind might get fuzzy
your head a little light
jive till the vinyl's spiral ends
and beyond if no one dares lift the arm
where the diamond tip and vinyl meet
c'est la vie, is what it is

Phenomenology is the study of the structures of consciousness as experienced from the first-person point of view. In phenomenology, evidence is limited to intuitive knowledge, often associated with the controversial assumption that it provides indubitable access to truth.

LOST IN TRANSLATION

Sadly, the evidence
was lost in translation
aptly, all proof
was lost in our passion

Sadly, the evidence
was lost in our ardour
duly, the testimony
was lost in our amour

Sadly, the evidence
was lost, cuz we were alone
gladly, the gospel
was lost, cuz we were error prone

Sadly, the evidence
was lost in our delusion
happily, the veracity
was lost, cuz we were human

What is evidence anyway
something that backs an overture
accepted to mean that the premise is pure
what is truth but something obscure
turned into something further blurred
blurted out in language both callow and absurd

Evidence backs belief
belief abets stance
an entrancing improvised dance
a view prized by a biased mind
created with our eyes closed
each time we conjugate

Bargara Dec 2024

It's seems natural when we first meet, that humans size each other up. Sarah Winman says that humans are spatially mid-way between an atom and a star. Some science geeks have actually calculated that the hippopotamus is more likely the midway point. This actually puts us behind the hippo if we use space as a metric. Not so impressive. Could this be why so many of us are driven to act more grandiose than we really are. Are we hiding from the fact that we are less than average.

MASKED BALL

Walking the tightrope
betwixt dare and caution
preying we
won't fall

Sweating bullets
no one sees
neath the mask, after all
this here's a masked ball

This hoedown
shows we all are
midway 'tween
an atom and a star

Life's lived
in a nowhere land
a gnarled mad mix
of woe, joy and irony

Hell is empty
all the devils are here
life's a feeding frenzy
a lawless frontier

Scurrilousness
is so delicious
be a fool
be capricious

The bard was right
the world is a stage
we're all actors
let's act out tonight

Let's make like a devil
or like a saint
what's the difference
underneath the war paint

Remember
we're troubadours
wardrobe and makeup
affords applause

Clapperboards
snap, act
larger than we are
tis what it's all about

"All the world's a stage, and all the men and women merely players." – William Shakespeare

This week, I learned that in Norse mythology, there is an elixir called Poetic Mead. It's a mythical beverage and whoever drinks it becomes a scholar able to recite any information and solve any question. The drink is a vivid metaphor for poetic inspiration, often associated with the god Odin. The writing of the following piece was ably assisted by a favourable Argentinian white wine.

MEDITATION

Emperor Aurelius
once kingpin in Rome
was better known as a philosopher

From all accounts he was beneficent
Marcus left us his note books
which remain magnificent

Many still use his quotes
as a moral compass
I'm one of those, I'll happily confess

Marcus markedly said
"Everything we see is a perspective,
not the truth."

My perspective is
that our brain's a finely primed
chemical soup

Jam packed with neurotransmitters
that create "perspective"
in my case, I once added some

These altered my outlook
for the better
until they didn't

My brain became a primordial bog
all was mundane, me an anhedonic log
in the end

Leary was a brave neuronaut
Tim tried pretty hard to cheat
that gloomy trend

Chemicals are neither good nor bad
but when they're used for
bad reasons, it's sad

I don't know if AI and Elon Musk's
robobots will bring a change
to anything

Today my perspective is gratitude
that I can breathe, I can connect,
I can serve others

Now nothing is mundane
In fact all is truly
awesome

I'm glad I probed, made to pivot
several times; after all growth
abhors a straight line

Now I might be wrong
I may have misunderstood
but who really cares

If the music's good, let's dance
let's do acroyoga, and meditate while
we have a chance

Note: **Marcus** Aurelius – Emperor of Rome (161–180 AD) and a Stoic philosopher.
Timothy Leary (1920–1996) American psychologist and author known for his strong advocacy of psychedelics.

Multivitamins and food supplements will give you expensive urine. Exercise, like riding a bicycle, will give you wellbeing.

PEDDLE PILL

Breeze feathers my face, I push through air
though not a race, I'm mindful of the rush
since I alone set the pace
I dance within, my soul shimmies to a song
music comes from above, choral tweets of merry banter
emits from birds peering down at me

A whiff of fine mist fixes an aroma
sniffing in the fresh wet fauna; sun in the background
I'm shaded by trees
my eyes coolly auditing a vast pallet of greens
the tints and tones and hues; this is what it's like
when I ride my bike

I banish dark reverie, flicking it aside
bad juju, junk baggage washes over me
I just ride
I peddle at a tempo I decide
'cuz I like feeling, hearing, smelling, seeing

all that is bright for me; all that is right

Push, peddle, push, like it's a wellness pill
lifestyle prescriptions aren't complimentary
they are the real deal

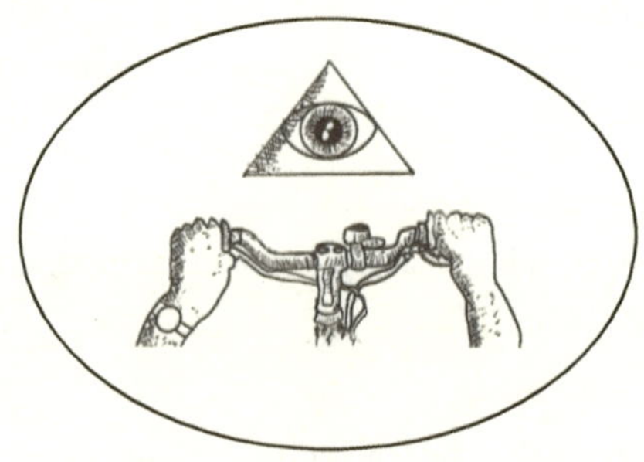

Bargara February 2023

Recently I learnt that a female cat was called a Queen. Of course, I knew that the male cat was a Tom. Suffice to say, it was terrific to discover that there was still essential knowledge out there that I could still discover.

QUEENS

Two cats sit
in a dim
smoke-hazed loft
downtown somewhere

Both with
stoney stance
nothing set
to chance

Each in
labelled black
lips red
articulate

Their jive
calm and steady
their table-talk
a rhapsody

The scene's so
avant-garde
you can't miss
the show

Two queens
complicit
defying
simplicity

It was more
than just
a meeting
of minds

There was a
head-on
rap of
stoic passions

The discourse
bold 'n' unflinching
dispersing wisdom of
their own making

Nothing fake
spoiled this landscape
just a desire
to reshape the universe

When
the confab's done
why not raise
a hindleg to the sky

and showing class
both cats proceed to
French kiss
their a**e

Bargara August 2025

Sarah Winman wrote Still Life, a hit novel in 2021. I am a member of the Tough Guy Book Club, Bundaberg Chapter, and Still Life was our tabbed read for March 2025. I was gripped by the author's ability to distil an exquisite testament to the impermanence of life, the many forms of love which exist and the value of art. This poem is my tribute.

STILL LIFE

The brevity
was never lost on me
life's calm turbulence
was cozy

Life's fleetingness
did not bother me
Its impermanence
did not frighten me

I honoured it
was not a casualty
life's conciseness
gave it whimsy

My moments
were delicious
my transitory story
may not be recall
yet is forever mine

There were moments
so astonishing
they stopped
the beating
of my heart

Disquiet when my
flaws were disclosed
goes to show
truth I suppose

Life holds
many forms of love
parental, lust
deep-rooted, abandoned
friendships based on trust

It will be over in a minute
so live while
there's Still Life

"Time is a precious gift. Use it wisely." Still Life by Sarah Winman

The term "overview effect" was coined by author Frank White in the 1980s. It refers to a cognitive shift reported by some astronauts while viewing the Earth from space. The most prominent aspects of personally viewing the Earth from space are appreciation and perception of beauty, unexpected and even overwhelming emotion, and an increased sense of connection to other people and the Earth as a whole.

"THE OVERVIEW EFFECT"

The best view, of the human race
comes from looking, down from space
seen from here, here on the moon
the earth's a tiny, blue ballon

Why does distance make for a clearer view
of our existence, what is that due to
is. the art of seeing so bizarre
that clarity comes only from afar

Raw emotions, connection us all
the blue ballon changes, our ideas for sure
pundits call it, "the overview effect"
when grownups renege, 'n reclaim a child's awe

Looking at a tiny orb, your diggings on a dot
camping at a place, once mostly gas
why say the earth's big, when it's plainly not
this "overview effect", dumbfounds astronauts

I don't know why, to this day
I feel my earth-home's, a cliché
the best view of, the human race
comes from looking, down from space

Michael Collins (Apollo 11;1969) said "the thing that really surprised me was that it [Earth] projected an air of fragility. And why, I don't know. I don't know to this day. I had a feeling it's tiny, it's shiny, it's beautiful, it's home, and it's fragile."

Bargara Oct 2024

There's always friction between form and function. We are born naked, yet are required to cover up. There's the function to stay warm and the function to adorn ourselves for our own identity or for seduction. It's all a little weird. I propose the contents of our dress up box be for both form or function.

THE TIGER BEETLE & THE FOX

The yoke
of fashion
aint a joke
whether
you're a woman
or a bloke

I'm sometimes
a beetle
sometimes
a symbol
a token
making a point

The yoke
of fashion
wears high heels
like spikes hanging
round your neck
drawing blood

The
Tiger Beetle
has style
its iridescence's so
you could wear it
as a brooch

Still
I'd rather
be shopping
right now
I'm a male diva
in training

Catch it
splay it
spray it with epoxy
the beetle
won't complain
it can't talk

A logo
runs across
my chest
branding
at its
very best

May I interject
there's grandeur
in self-reproach
a fox makes a chic shawl
why not
a Tiger Beetle broach

The business of the poet and the novelist is to show the sorriness underlying the grandest things and the grandeur underlying the sorriest things. Thomas Hardy (1840–1928)

Tiger Beetles, one of the most colourful beetles, have iridescent shells.

I have noticed that mankind's lifetime is a sequence of nows and they are limited. Theophrastus, an ancient Greek philosopher, naturalist and a colleague of Aristotle's said: *"Time is the most valuable thing a man can spend."* Hence, my call to arms "make time for time".

TIME-4-TIME

Let each moment liquify, embrace its show-n-tell
bathe in its fluidity, let it soak you and enthral
sway but stay completely still, wallow in timelessness
stand naked in the sacred pool, get wet, float in it all

Wade through the waterscape, foray into the feeling
venture for adventure's sake, flow on for you'll be safe
be inspired or be incensed as you trek the mystique
you may not get what you want, but you'll find the crucial place

Listen to the music, a soundtrack to the here and now
with its harmonies and rhythms, as the sounds coalesce somehow
mark the melody in your being, traipse each candid phrase
crisscross the manuscript, go lightly as you leaf each page

Hold no certainties, they'll just scuttle your soul
don't concern yourself with things you can't control
own the option to let things be
mind is an enigma, opinions mere distractions, leave them alone

Tour the instant, as you would ride each breath
right-on the joyride, let hallelujah reign
swallow and be swallowed, plunge its depths
make time4time, over and again

Sentosa Island, Singapore May 2023

I compare memories with my brother occasionally and often there is variance. Then I stumbled upon this quote: *"We now know that memories are not fixed or frozen, like Proust's jars of preserves in a larder, but are transformed, disassembled, reassembled, and recategorized with every act of recollection."* – Oliver Sacks, neurologist, author (1933–2015). It's up to us all to uncover the roots, rifts and collective restraint of memory.

WHY NOT

To all your answers
I'll match a question
each of your memories
I'll tag a lie

To your every want
I'll counter with a need
you want a song
I'll play it in silence

Doctrine to you
it's only a flashback
you captured this
I'll hand you back that
promise me I
won't turn out normal
hell, who'd ever want that

The song you hear
will help you understand
the song you catch
won't need an answer

Some say you need
to first learn the rules
'fore you can start
breaking 'em

You say why
I say why not
simply make 'em
angle, aspect
listening to learn
attitude, context
not to reply

Tell me why
Tell me what
Tell me why
Tell me why not

To your every rule
I'll make a caveat
you will break 'em
trump that, I make 'em

You say why
I say why not
simply make 'em
angle, aspect
listening to learn
attitude, context
not to reply

Tell me why

The largest wind chime I have ever seen is in Barcaldine, Queensland, Australia. It houses "The Tree of Knowledge". Put it on your bucket list. Make sure you see it on a windy day. It inspired me to write these lyrics about tribalism.

WIND CHIME

Dance – to a descant wind chime
In step – with a mystic drum
Move – to velvet music
Brave it – it is so much fun
Trip – to the light fantastic
Raid – your own intimate space
Blink – all other comms denied
Fly high – plant a smile on your face
Tango – to the noise of the tempest
Cavort – to god's metronome
Tread – to the buzz inside your head
Boogie – like you're on your own
Dart – to the up-tempo mambo
Flutter – like a boxer in a ring
Flirt – as a lithe belly dancer would
Sway – like you control everything
Bop – like the beat has merit
Float – in praise of this reign
Wander – let your soul meander
Hover – let's hangout again
Strut – like you're a cockfight pilot
Prance – like you just can't dance

Chant – cuz you've found your tribe
Shimmy – like there's no tomorrow

True Knowledge is a Wind Chime with Chaos at it's Sacred Circle as an Epic Dance

---

Barcaldine July 2021

AUSTRALIANNA

The Outback KN

There's something great about a music festival. I think it's the licence that allows you to let your own freak-flag fly. In a world that mostly pushes orthodoxy, it's a relief to be who you really wanna be, even if just for a moment. A chance to raid the inner child's dress-ups box and give the bird to normal. The festival that I reflect upon was in Agnes Water (2021), but could have been anywhere.

AGNES WATER FREAKSHOW

When the minstrel troop came to town, we-all cut loose
'twas a psycho's license to dress up like freakshow clowns
we loved the way it all went down

Agnes became a landing pad, a voyeur's utter paradise
with acolytes to the right of us, flunkies to the left
protégés and émigrés for the rest

There were wannabees, and a whole horde more
human flotsam and jetsam all washed up
upon this screwball sandy shore

There were no types spared, even the Devil was there
He and Jesus spoke heart to heart
both had so much shit to share

Both buried the hatchet, declaring a truce for the fair
they loosened their grip on each other's throat
then chugalugged an ice-cold beer

Lots of lively chatter 'tween the inked-up Vets
those from our first nations; cowgirls cooed with savoir faire
while others grooved with a vacant stare

When the minstrel troop came to town, we-all cut loose
'twas a psycho's license, to dress up like freakshow clowns
we loved the way it all went down

"The world is all the richer for having a devil in it, so long as we keep our foot upon his neck." – William James

Bargara Feb 2025

These words were inspired by a road trip across central Australia.

DUST DEVIL

A dinky
dust devil, wields an
unseen broom, affectionately
sweeping with blank nonchalance.
I was never more, happy, and alone
than when I found myself out of
my comfort zone
tomorrow come the dawn
let's go on and discover
new shades of
sky blue

A roadside mallee tree
is dutifully shaken like a weathercock
rules direction of travel. Along the Plenty
Highway, we came upon a vine
bearing strange fruit
that could be the
death of me.

I was never more,
happy, and alone than when I
found myself, out of my comfort zone.
tomorrow come the dawn let's go on
and discover new shades of
sky blue.

Zebra finches
dart on mass in gold-olive
mulga scrub, their behaviour
deep-rooted and chaperoned by song.
I was never more, happy, and alone than
when I found myself out of my
comfort zone.

Larapinta July 2021

In May 1891, it is said that at least 3000 striking shearers protested against poor working conditions and low wages paid by the landed sheep farming gentry in Barcaldine, Queensland. The leaders hatched a plan for the first real labour war beneath the boughs of a ghost gum tree. The tree subsequently earned the name *The Tree of Knowledge*. This shearers' strike is credited as being one of the main drivers leading to for the formation of the Australian Labor Party.

GHOST GUM

A ghost gum let
the shearers see
what clearly lay
beyond the tree

Journeymen and gentry
were warring over pay
battlelines were drawn
in Barcaldine that day

Neither were to be denied
what both knew
they were due
as terms were pressed
and in turn voided
the ghost gum sighed a
"why"

All that mattered
is what became
of the lively game
called politics

All that matters
is whether you choose
the carrot
or the stick

That sage of a tree
became a refugee twice
once to love
once to loathing

Journeymen and gentry
were warring
over pay
battlelines were drawn
in Barcaldine
that day

The *Knowledge Tree*
chanced it to say
we could all
do better

The Tree of Knowledge

Barcaldine Sept 2021

Banjo Paterson penned the lyrics to *Waltzing Matilda* in 1895. His bush ballad has been described as Australia's "unofficial national anthem". History records that the lyrics were penned in Winton, Queensland. Back then, itinerant workers travelled on foot and referred to their swag or belongings as Matilda. Jump forward to today and most, travel in a ute. This poem is a tribute to and my attempt at scribing a modern version of the much loved song.

MATILDA & ME

Head down jumbuck
lay low an' zip it
we could be in a ruckus
for trouble is near
I'll try a backhander
but should the baksheesh
not cut it
I'll gun this crate an' rocket
right outta here

Could be a cluster-fuck
closing in up ahead
no time to waltz
no spell to meddle
should the troopers
not wanna play nice
I'll plant a fiend led boot
square on the pedal

Swagman, bagman
I've been called many things
with my pack in the back
of my ute named Bluey
my life to this point
has been charmed indeed
Lady Luck and me
have been tagging a beauty

Hello Banjo, rattle my bones
cos Bluey, Max and me
travel oh so free

I don't do no
hot billy tea
that steamy black water
won't hack it with me
my thing is wine
drunk from a Vegemite jar
to the brim, make it cold
make it a cheeky Chablis

I'm a traveling man
I wield an axe
a battered old tanbur
that I call Max
with just five strings strung
I strum and I warble
lyrics I've penned
it helps the wildlife relax

Come dusk I'm headed
for my fave camp site
and guess what, son
I'm eatin' lambchops tonight
hell yeah, and why not
with so many out there
surely I won't
be begrudged
just one, am I right

Hello Banjo, rattle my bones
cos Bluey, Max my and me
travel oh so free

Winton July 2021

Satin Bowerbirds are found along most of the eastern and south-eastern coast of Australia. The males are renowned for decorating their bowers with all manner of blue objects collected from the vicinity of the bower and sometimes from farther afield. These odds and ends may comprise feathers from parrots, flowers, seed pods, fruits, butterfly wings and artificial items such as ball-point pens, matchboxes, string, marbles and pieces of glass. Basically the males pilfer stuff to attract a mate. I wonder, is male chicanery a wider thing.

SATIN BOWERBIRD

How's my tab
at the last count
how did I come
to this nest
stealing bits
and bobs to build
to best furnish
this alluring home

A shrine of colour
a temple of sanctuary
a safe haven
a place of beauty

My base bricks
are always sticks
my cladding's
anything blue
come mate
with me

Fixated to a tee
Ptilonorhynchus V
I'm a thief with self-belief
never shamed
a pimpernel
a Valentine
wholeheartedly
self-proclaimed

A stolen peg
a broken thong
all of the same
true blue

A hallowed place
a shrine of sanctuary
a safe blue haven
a thing of beauty
come mate
with me

Hamilton Island Nov 2021

My wife spoils me. She always seems to find an amazing experience as a birthday present. In 2022, it was 90 minutes hooning in an chauffeur driven premium classic wooden speed boat. I felt like James Bond crossing Lake Como. There's nothing like a champaign in hand, wind in your hair, cuddling up with the love of your life without a care and playing to the imagination of your inner twelve year old.

WOW-CATION

Our runabout raised its bow
tilting in tune to a Volvo hum
we were stepping up the pace

Wake-waves countered tactfully
gifting us an aerosol
with a cool salty taste

To a reassuring shudder
we skimmed olive green water
in this, our mahogany flying fish

Such WOW worthy grandeur
so wonderful for us, the lucky few
as we blew off our mind's cobwebs

Cuz that's what you do on a wow-cation

Noosa Jan 2022

HISTORY and THE CLASSICS

I met Andrea, a moxie musician in mid-2023. She dropped into a meeting at our local poetry club. Rather than recite a poem, Andrea played an original piece on her viola. Closing my eyes, my stream of consciousness commissioned this melancholic tale of a woe, of whalers' widows left behind.

1849

Once I held
a seashell
near my ear
and heard a choir
of wailing widows
mourning men
who'd set to sea
to harvest whales

Seeing these men
scorning life
the ocean consorted
often siding with the whales
wantonly swallowing
countless men
wherefore many of them
did not come home

I wonder
if this woe
of weeping sisters
cried for their forfeited men
or was it in lieu
of the lunacy of mammal-man
cuz after all
whales are mammals too

Inspired by an untitled solo viola piece played by Andrea Viola Boss

As far as we know, humans first evolved in Africa, and much of early human expansion occurred on that continent. In the early 70s, I recall attending a Osibisa (a Ghanaian-British Afro-rock band founded in the late 1960) concert. They started their set off with "we gonna start these happy vibes right from the root, and the root is early one morning in the heart of Africa. We call this the Dawn". We are so lucky to be able to experience a new dawn each day.

DAWN

The first hint of skylight, just 'fore sunrise
is what we call the dawn; it marks when
the day is born

If you wake up and breathe, it's already a try
fuck all other matters that wanna nullify the awe
and suck you dry

Morning dread's a weird fear that wants us to don
The rags of prey; just leave your bed yet keep
your JBF hair on

Repeatedly our ID carps bout what might be lost
when our magic carpet ride could end
but who gives a toss

Unsure of what's coming next, why do we forget
to ask life's key question, which is what have
we not done yet

Dawn occurs every day; when no one knows
what harbour they're making for who cares anyway
let's go make hay

The first hint of skylight, just 'fore sunrise
is what we call the dawn and that's when
all is awe, a raw surprise, the birth of a new day
let's go make hey

"When a man does not know what harbour he is making for, no wind is the right wind." – Seneca

The power of the Shōgun was reliant on the Samurai who lived life according to the Bushido code of conduct. Bushido required not fearing death and dying for valour. From my readings, it glorifies the moment between life and death as the essence that denotes when living is fiercely real. It insinuated that living on that razor's edge is the only true way to revere existence. I don't know if I agree but it's certainly an interesting perspective, in some ways equating life to a haiku, or a transient piece of exquisite origami. There is a similarity in the Viking warrior code. Mankind is kinda weird.

SHŌGUN

Chilling in a hot tub, purring as geishas tout
singing lilting songs, something to be aroused about
within the calm waters, the surface veneer glistening
exquisitely inky blue, like a phosphorescent snakeskin

We stepped out from the water, wholly reawakened
if we die tonight, I loved the ride, for I was me
all other souls were taken
Our satire is a form of art to help us tell farce apart
from the only thing that's vital, a parent's smile
true from their heart

The presence of a mastermind would not stop this war
or this dance, broiling in a hot tub
forming life and death's romance

1,2,3,4 what are we fighting for, given half a chance
we might escape the earthquake
but not this life… this avalanche
our story wrapped in life-speed nanoseconds of glory

Like many, I was engrossed by the coverage of the November 2024 US presidential elections. It seems to me that American voters love vaudeville. And I have to admit that Trump is a great comic showman. I doubt that the President-elect is smart, but he's smart enough to buy a great "read the room crew." Trump is a modern Druid.

THE MAN

The troupe arrive
in high-volt form
surrounding the Dude
his savvy minders
his read-the-room crew
his paladin brood

They speedily
set to work
listening-n-noting
passing on to him
the mood
of the gathering

For years his horde
honed their skills
amping his ability
to amuse-n-hike
his proclivity
to schmooze

They gave the Dude
the gallery view
to mirror back
play to the pack
with mostly non-verbal cues
he's fab at that

His mostly tacit lines
bang on point
always the giver
firing back
the in-vogue vibe
the crowd would quiver

It's a skill
been drilled
over time
polished to perfection
constantly
refined

The Dude can
pivot and deliver
his message
his demeanour
quite curated for
the right culture fit

Some call it charisma
others pizazz
or is it mesmerism
maybe the Dude
is really a Druid
or just The Man

"Nature affords a universal means of healing and preserving men." – Franz Anton Mesmer

Cockaigne or Cockayne is a land of plenty in medieval myth, an imaginary place of luxury and ease, comfort and pleasure, opposite to the harshness of medieval peasant life. Spoiler alert, the turtle is my totem.

THE ROAD TO COCKAIGNE

Ms Turtle
flicked sand
into my face
purposefully
but not on purpose

Her action
set me dreaming
bout something
counterfeit
yet legitimate

Her move
made sense
like silence
adds to music
my dream too
was bountiful

That flick
moved her an inch
but me
I moved a mile
or more

This Ms
is a talisman
dusting sand
into my eyes
casting a spell

Her action
propelled me
to Cockaigne
her gesture
a sign to
delight again

I recently joined the *Tough Guys Book Club*. The novel for the month was *The Secret History*, by Donna Tartt (1992). For me it's a tale of youthful fantasy and curiosity as experienced by those privileged enough to attend a liberal university, and eager to imbibe in hedonistic pleasures. Unfortunately, when things go bad, they go very bad. The moral is that unbridled hedonism can lead to lethal secrets that rarely end well.

THE SECRET HISTORY

This *Secret History*
tells the story
of a sub-genre
of olden academia
where a professor
with an odd proclivity
claims the right to hand-pick
his student coterie

Their privileged mien
only so
in warped
semi-pecuniary terms
their mystique
their difference
their aesthetic appeal
was festering with worms

Something's happening
pencils are being sharpened
have your erasers ready
cuz you might need them
there may be memories
or someone you'll need
to rub out like
a *Secret History* no doubt

Enter Dionysia
the ecstatic bacchanal
and the decay
that it brings
yoo-hoo to the hunter
who preys upon them
as puppet master
pulling the strings

In the end
for these chosen few
it all turns to shit
depleted and trapped
in a miasma
when guilt hits
and finally destroys
the once tight crew

Something's happening
pencils are being sharpened
have your erasers ready
cuz you might need them
there may be memories
or someone you'll need
to rub out like
a *Secret History* no doubt

"Icarus flew too close to the sun, but at least he flew." – Jeremy Robert Johnson.

It's sad that many live in perpetual external peril. Just as sad is that there are those whose peril is an internal construct, the result of an inner critic hell bent on causing a constantly catastrophic state. Even the slightest emotion, triggers a shutdown of rational thought and cognitive dissonance descends to cripple them. These folk live beneath a Sword of Damocles. [The Sword of Damocles hanging over your head, means that they are in a situation in which something very bad could happen at any time]. But there is always hope of a mindset redemption, as this poem demonstrates.

THE SWORD

Years ago
when my mortal life began
I sensed trust was missing
in my makeup as a man

Why this obsession
oh such pain
why all this conflict
searing my brain

In a word
the Sword of Damocles
hung menacingly
over my head

Karma came
with her solution
she handed me autonomy
to make me understand

She threw me a cue
the mindset I needed
her words struck a chord
something I've since heeded

Life's made
by a two-edged blade
Karma's words were a billboard
Saying that I was The Sword

The wrong one in
the Kings Chair
sits beneath The Sword
strung up by a strand of hair

While the rightful one
as their reward
transcends to become
that very Sword

With that reframe
and now being The Sword
I cut myself from myself
to connect with the world

Now I am
The Sword of Damocles
Now I am
The Sword

I have Dutch-Norse ancestry. My parents called me Kees, the Dutch diminutive of Cornelius. In primary school, my teachers said Kees sounded too strange. They "anglicised" Kees to Keith. In secondary school, Kees still was too foreign, so my teachers called me Con. That would have been okay had I'd been Irish. The irony is that Ireland was once ruled by the Vikings. I had blue eyes and blonde hair. God knows how this would have played out if my skin and hair were dark. Bloodlines serve oppressors. Humanity is inter-related. Racism is a scientifically dubious; a woo-woo manmade construct.

WOO-WOO

Once upon a time
Zahara came
to live
among us

Zahara was
previously
just a bird
in a tree

And every day
Zahara walked the line
completely calm
nonplussed

Fearless of
a breaking branch
her wings bracing
her self-belief

Until one day
someone made a play
on her way home
on the school bus

Until the play
blew
her faith
away

And because of that
she came to be
ashamed
of her bloodline

'Til finally
Zahara flipped
the fake storyline
drama woo-woo

Drama woo-woo
drama woo-woo
Who am I
drama woo-woo
drama woo-woo
who are you

Ever since
that day
Zahara had the grit to say
drama woo-woo
this is me
who are you

"A bird sitting in a tree is not afraid of the branch breaking,
because her trust is not in the branch, but in her wings." – Anonymous.

Bargara July 2025

TRAVEL and EXPLORATION

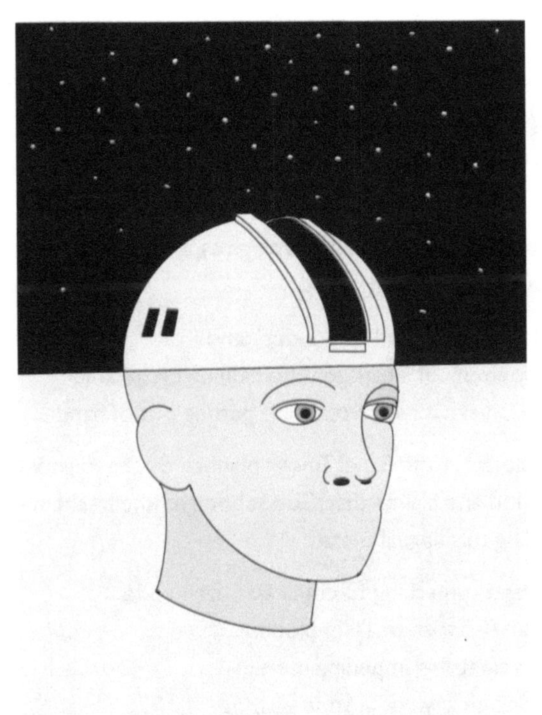

The Hitchhiker's Guide to the Galaxy (Douglas Adams, 1978) describes a device called a babel fish. It provides an instant translations of any dialect across the galaxy. I participated in a Digital Strategy meeting recently. There were digital architects, clinicians, financial folk and executive managers. The discussion was going nowhere. Having been born without a filter, I raised my hand and asked if we could all be provided with babel fish. I got an applause.

BABEL FISH

Quick, I need a babelfish so I can understand
the cacophony of languages is a puzzling broadband
the vocab and syntax are entirely out of hand

One guy over there is talking poison
hoping someone else view will die
or have I misunderstood the wrangling coming from him

Everywhere there's weird shit, shame, blame, psychic scars
feelings that are far beyond the spoken word
all expressed by noise and tones that sound absurd

I need to connect and while our non-verbals are shared
words still provide a nuance that gives a clue to
the state of mind being aired

I need a babelfish so I can understand
the cacophony of languages, the baffling broadband
the foreign syntax and vocab are getting out of hand

The fable 'bout the Babel Tower planned by the mighty clans
of Babylon and claims that God sabotaged their scheme
by making this lingual mess

Still, I need something to crack this darn code
I need an AI assist, or I'll implode;
there's something impeding me
I can't decipher what anyone's saying
what kindda game is God playing

"A different language is a different vision of life." – Federico Fellini

---

Brisbane May 2024

Half of us are nomads. Global demographics suggests the other half will marry and live within a few kilometres of their birthplace. Nomads will migrate and make new homes on the other side of this planet earth. The Australian Bureau of Statistics Census Data (2021) confirms that more than half of Australian residents were either born overseas or have a parent born overseas. This is a poem inspired by a conversation with a random stranger in a coffee shop in Alice Springs. She came to Australia from Germany on a working visa. What kind of nomad will Charlie choose to be.

CHARLIE

Charlie's eyes beamed confidence, like diamonds wise to their worth
I's curious to know what she'd hitherto seen and now more mindfully saw

Charlie 'd spent time in the outback 'round Alice "on country"
mixing with First Nations' mobs, living a life both rich and raw

Charlie bore no pretence, secure in her own skin
yet like most of us, now and then, she'd an innate pain to rein in

Charlie 'd been born in the Rhineland, came to Oz at eighteen
in ten years she'd learnt a lot, not leaving much in the NT unseen

Her bio-clock was ticking, where to lay her bloodline now front of mind
return to the lands of her roots or find new blood in a place far from home

Charlie unburdened, I listened and validated, who was I to interfere
still my question was: what lies at the heart of Charlie's heartache
each and every human is one of a greater us, joined by the same blood
same descent; give me a break we're all from the same mother earth

I'm sure Charlie will return to the Rhine, I also suspect she'll return
this country's a seductress. God Bless you Charlie, go and come back
to the outback 'round Alice to live a great life both rich and so much more

"As used in the modern world, *both race and ethnicity remain social constructs*;
neither term delineates genetic or biological categories." – TB Mersha

Alice Springs Feb 2025

I revel in making mistakes. I aim to make three a day. That way I can reassure myself that I'm learning something. So this statement might be a mistake. For some time I have believed that the best return on investment vis-à-vis education is travel. Travel reveals just how confined our bias-bubble can be.

JESTER

She was the jester
with an X-factor
willfully mixing
comedy with fact

Recklessly hatching
daft ideas
blind and unruly
yet exact

The give-and-take of
the interplay
was directed by demons
produced out of joy
she was never
the smartest one
in the room

If she thought
she might be
she scurried on
for she was the jester
just having fun
with everyone

Her rally cry was
read science for facts
and fiction for truth
give it a try
travel and be a jester
a mindful couch surfer

Ever the critic
her art was her joy
her happy place
or so, it seemed

Blasting holes in truth
was her frolic
praise was what
she played on

In a carnival
it's hard not to flee
down game alley
to feel free

The give-and-take of
the interplay was
directed by demons
produced out of joy
She was never
the smartest person
in the room

Those street smart
with a duffle bag
who travelled
far and wide
fared much better
than the nailed down kids
it's really that simple
travel and be a jester

"The world is a book, and those who do not travel read only one page." – Saint Augustine

Living in Sydney meant that anywhere we had to travel, was a one hour car trip in congested and palpably hostile traffic, each way. I was over it so my family relocated to Bundaberg in regional Queensland in 1999. Twenty-five years later, I have had no regrets. We sometimes travel to Sydney, but fly down, catch a train to the CBD, stay in a nice hotel and walk everywhere, or perhaps catch a ferry. After three days of a big-city fix, we cheerfully return home. I'm a Sydney refugee, now blissfully free from the terrorism inflicted by big-city traffic. I was remined of this over Easter when one man's aggravation, brought the six-laned Bruce Highway to a virtual stop for three hours. Thank God I don't drive in Jakarta or Mumbai!

TRAFFIC REFUGEE

The ride was chaotic
our nerves unravelled
each inch of asphalt
commandeered by cars

The hustle and bustle
left us nowhere to retreat
each escape route
barred by steel on rubber

Eager to move
but going nowhere
this traffic had
something to prove

We were all so close
but far from intimate
there was no connection
only conniption

Who needs chaos
it's sheer bedlam
let's turn
the clock back

The joy of travel
by auto is fading
let's return to walking
or ride a bike

Take the route less travelled
the path less peopled
travel defines us
not concrete and tar

Road rage
has become extensive
here's my missive
let's get out of here

Inuit are Indigenous people of the Arctic. The word Inuit means "the people" in the Inuit language. I cannot help but respect them for surviving in such harsh conditions. They graciously allow us as strangers into their small communities. Travel teaches Cultural Intelligence to those who wish to seek it.

WELCOME TO COUNTRY

Welcome to country
we acknowledge you
please remember to
wipe your feet
before you enter

For those who don't know
that's a synonym
to leave all afore
prejudice
at the door

Don't enter
with an ego
enter as a child
with eyes and ears open
with awe

Each day
let us pray
that all of us are
okay, connected
and thriving

First people
second people
third people, I don't care
so long as
respect is there

Diversity needs
to be embraced
all "isms"
should to be
ignored

They're all
slings and arrows
and ought to be
cast aside
cuz all are flawed

Once again
welcome to country
please remember
wipe your feet
before you enter

LOVE and INTIMACY

Delia

Aristotle wrote: "Man is by nature a social animal; an individual who is unsocial naturally and not accidentally is either beneath our notice or more than human. Society is something that precedes the individual. Anyone who either cannot lead the common life or is so self-sufficient as not to need to, and therefore does not partake of society, is either a beast or a god." Many argue this is his most famous quote. Yet, we fall asleep, dream, wake up, inhabit our skin, and experience our liminal conscious state alone. Quite the irony.

ALONE

Am I the only one who wakes up alone
am I the only one who loves the morning birdsong
the only one who's in awe when the day creeps in
am I the only one whose solitude creates a smile within

At the end of the day, the sun goes down
at the end of the day, we are all alone
even with our soulmate and lover
we are both alone
we're alone together

Am I the only one that breathes for only me
am I the only one who hums when I'm alone
in a sea of everything, I am just a wink
my aloneness is a touchstone
best of all, we're alone together

Are you the only one who wakes up alone
are you the only one who loves the break of day
the only one who's grateful to a spirit in the sky
coz best of all, we're here alone together

When the sun goes down
at the end of the day
even with my soulmate and lover
curled up next to me
I am, you are, we're both alone
yet best of all, we're alone together

Asherah was a major goddess in ancient Northern Semitic cultures, which includes modern-day Syria, Lebanon, Jordan, Israel, and Palestine, as well as parts of northern Mesopotamia. Asherah was associated with fertility, motherhood, and sacred trees. She was sometimes called the "progenitress of the gods". Some scholars have suggested that Asherah was the predecessor of the Christian Eve, hence morphing into the "progenitress of original sin". Call me dull, but I fail to see anything original about sin.

ASHERAH

Albeit born
with shame and guilt
I ditched 'em quick
before I'd wilt
their bearing on me
wholly contested

Asherah said
it's your body
your mind
your choice
Her call to arms
came time-tested

It's She who made
that which exists
because She preyed
It persists...
Asherah cared
n was invested

Maybe She would dance with me
maybe take a chance
after midnight, when the wolves
come circling
we'd be hurtling towards infinity
with confidence
we'd surely meld to each other well
or at least her to me!

"Even their children remember their altars and Asherah poles beside the spreading trees on high hills." - Jeremiah-17:2

Bargara Nov 2025

Hellelil and Hildebrand, the Meeting on the Turret Stairs is a painting by Frederic William Burton, from 1864. The art work depicts the love story of Hellelil who fell in love with her personal guard Hildebrand. The story was taken from a medieval Danish ballad translated as *Hellalyle and Hildebrand*. Spoiler alert: it didn't end well. In 2012, the painting was voted by the Irish public as Ireland's favourite art work. My poem/song lyric, is inspired by that work.

HELLELIL and HILDEBRAND

We villainously met
in a covert stairwell
your chiffon dress
a chic show and tell

We whispered all night
in clandestine time
I fell in love
yielding to your spell

We sang together
stories
of our amour
entangling us even more

Coupled by connection
footprints in the sand
walking talking
till we at last joined hands

We blatantly bungled
and silently fumbled
we unlocked "us"
With L plates on

Our paths were a river
raging at times
still at others
serpentine

We sang together
stories
of our amour
entangling us even more

And then it was over
all gone
we were no longer
we moved on

Reference: 'Hellelil and Hildebrand, the Meeting on the Turret Stairs' by Frederic William Burton, 1864

Our world confuses happiness for meaning. Love isn't always soft or simple; it's showing up when it's hard, choosing the same person even when the easy thing is to quit. Because at the end of a life, you won't remember the perfect days. You'll remember the storms you survived together.

NIRVANA

It was like any other
nuptial rite
the host stood up
n gave a toast
she smiled, took a
long deep breathe
looked at the couple
then directly at me, and said
I hope this wedding
will weather many storms
I hope in 40 years from now
you'll come to bless them
we all laughed
but later that night
as the music faded
and the crowd thinned
I sat and thought
about the "storms."
cuz my truth is
that's where love forms
I met my muse
she was twenty-one
I's slightly older
we had fun
but beyond the façade
we were both
kinda broken
but hey, we'd mime a grin
that'd outshine
a summer's day

We were frayed
broke n blissfully
unaware of what
real love would cost
the first few years
were fine
we built a tiny life
one argument at a time
then the
storms rolled in
I can't begin to
even describe them
nights when we
couldn't speak
days when
our mutual stupidity
turned into
full-on animosity
yet we never
gave up
cuz truth is that's
where love lies
it would've
been easy
to walk away
to find ourselves
but truth is
storms are where love lives
where love grows
where love turns into nirvana

"Marriage isn't about finding someone who makes you happy every day. It's about finding who's worth hurting with and healing with." – Linda Carter (Restful)

The song 'Polly Put the Kettle On' was published by Joseph Dale in Dublin around 1800. The nursery rhyme is mentioned in Charles Dickens' *Barnaby Rudge* (1841), which is the first record of the lyrics in their modern form. In 18th C middle-class families 'Sukey' was equivalent to 'Susan' and Polly was a pet-form of Mary. In 2025, I thought Suki was a cooler way to spell Sukey, and as she is now more mature, she may have moved beyond just playing tea parties with her BFF. These are my lyrics to a revised song.

SUKI

Suki take me tout suite, be my funky acrobat
blanket me with your lust, make-a-me your love-rat
Suki take me into your hollow, haul me down into the deep
Suki take me any which way, but do please do it tout suite

Suki move me, rock me gently; then slowly quicken the pace
evert your eyes then ogle me back; stare right at me face-to-face

Make me feel warm and cosy, I promise to reciprocate
we will make each moment last longer, let's celebrate
be both up and upside down, celebrities in our own minds
dressed in nothing at all
you my dear are my new wave, doing the best that you can
scintillating and radiant, I do enjoy the way you behave
let us both be primates; be funky monkey mates

Suki take me immédiatement, be my acrobat
blanket me with your true love, make-a-me your love-rat

Suki take me into your hollow, haul me down into your deep
Suki take me any which way, but do please do it tout suite
Suki move me, rock me gently, then slowly quicken the pace
evert your eyes then ogle at me, stare right at me face-to-face

Make me feel warm and cosy, I promise to reciprocate
we will make each moment last longer and celebrate

Polly put the kettle on, we'll all have tea. Sukey take it off again, they've all gone away.

Bargara Nov 2025

It was only a movie and thus a fiction. But I recently watched *A Complete Unknown*. I was captured by Sylvie Russo's doomed efforts to keep her love for Bob Dylan afloat. Walking away doesn't mean you've lost, it simply means that you've chosen yourself. Sylvie chose herself. I would imagine this is a common scenario in our early attempts at finding a soulmate.

TREADING WATER

How's this cosy chat
so far working out for you
please help me find out if
we're still on track
please do

Am I
missing something
you'd like to say
do you feel uneasy
in any way

Here's the thing
maybe I love you
but it's sure tiring
ever treading water
take the
chill factor down
the vibe in this room's
moving from warm to frosty

Too much ice
and one of us
could slip
into a crevasse
loss of trust is costly

This here's a dance for two
I can't read the signs
the subtle cues
all my questions hope to
stop things from turning blue

What were you hoping
we'd do today
in this life of uncertainty
I promise to listen more
and share the burden

When I sense things
are getting frosty, I won't
stick my head in the snow
or ask 'bout the weather
I'll zhush up
my wording
my gaze
my zilch ways

Here's the thing
maybe I love you
but it's
sure tiring
ever treading water

"Tis better to have loved and lost than never to have loved at all." – Alfred Tennyson.

GRATITUDE

KN

AVATAR

I'm smart, urbane, complex and torn
I love talking shit with random strangers
then again, I was born
to relish spending time alone

My childhood wasn't perfect, my folks were poles apart
their own youths marred by a war that skewed what they saw
"their own" survival plans became their sole perspective
and "their ownness" made them cursed from the start

The covert clues I got from them were obscure
I did and didn't know them, my views were jaded
does anyone really know anyone for sure
our psyches run deep and are well barricaded

I have all the necessities
I've had breathtakingly good luck
and when I learnt that lies masquerade as memories
waves of gratitude, began drenching each day

I accept there're those who had it worse
still the grit I have was shaped by anguish
being a sensitive child, can be a curse
in a sense, I'm the same as everyone

None of us know who we really are
what does it mean to be true to one's soul
could be we're all just an avatar
maybe that's life's goal

avatar (Reference: Thesaurus.com)

1. Hinduism. the descent of a deity to the earth in an incarnate form or some manifest shape; the incarnation of a god.

2. an embodiment or personification, as of a principle, attitude, or view of life:

Bargara Jan 2024

My wife and I were flying between Dubai and Copenhagen when it came to me just how fortunate I have been in the 71 years of my life. My gratitude was magnified by virtue of the fact that when I was 24 years old, I was seriously suicidal for four days following a hellishly traumatic incident at work. I am acutely aware that life is unfair. I am also aware that what almost killed me, made me who I now am. This poem had its genesis at that moment when I was eight miles high.

EIGHT MILES HIGH

Floating on a flatbed, eight miles high
a throw over my head, as I traverse the sky
digesting fine cuisine, my body's noncommittal
yet my mind's on standby, and here's why

Chrysalised, I focus on the sounds
as we scud around this small earth at large
there's the whining of the turbines
there's the air pummelling the fuselage

I wonder what Buddha would make of this
a mindful meditation, a grateful reflection of now
coz forty years or so ago, all my mind could debate
was my own annihilation, can you relate

For four days straight, my sole intention
was to bash into a tree and be dead and thus free
from the voice inside my head that said "son,
you'll never be good enough, so stop pretending"

After four days of the crazies, some angels came
to this day I don't know why
they saved me so I could have an awesome life
three fantastic kids and an amazing wife

Floating on a flatbed, business class
my body's noncommittal, but my mind's on standby
why was I favoured, so blessed, why, oh why
now eight miles high, how come I was the lucky one

"Culture can be healthy or toxic, nurturing or murderous" – Tom Hartmann

Bargara Oct 2024

I recall attending a "Welcome to Country" ceremony. The Elder delivered a missive that left me agog. She revealed that she was born in Cherbourg, Queensland, and was adopted at birth by a couple from Melbourne, both German academics. They provided unconditional love, and encouraged her to be curious and creative. She completed university studies and was well travelled globally. What astonished me, was when she said that she did not consider herself to be a part of "the stolen generation", but rather "the saved generation". Sometimes it takes a global village to raise a child. This Elder had navigated her mob, her clan, her nation, and the world's cultures. I was in awe.

WHO AM I – I'M ME

What's it mean
to be adopted
should I fuss
over why

Parentage
is a strange brew
in some cases
hard to apply

I came plainly
from conception
could that be down to
random selection

Kinda like
kids dropping
per chance
from a production line

The fountainhead
that bore me
defaulted in their task
to teach me to how to fly

Who am I, I know
who I am, I'm me

You can lose
the birth lottery
and still win
the lottery of life

My "true" parents
were a windfall
who wanted, loved
and made me whole

I'm blessed
to have no recall
and faint interest
in narrow heritage

In my mind
my adoption
meant I won
the lottery of life

What's it mean
to be adopted
should I fuss
over petty lineage

Who am I, I know
who I am, I'm me

It is not the honour that you take with you, but the heritage you leave behind – Branch Rickey.

INNER CHILD and OTHER FAIRY TALES

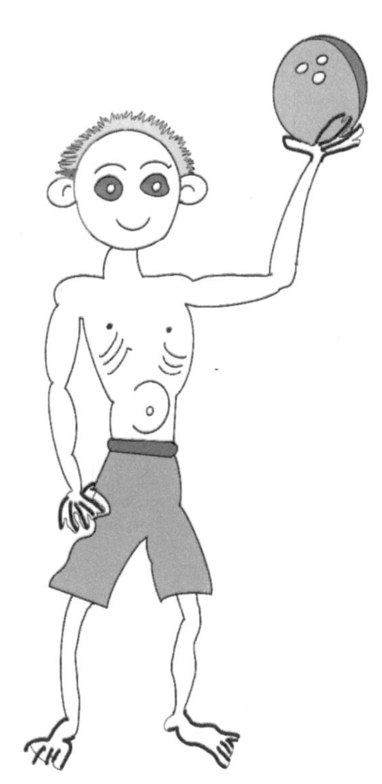

Albert Einstein said "Two things are infinite: the universe and human stupidity; and I'm not sure about the universe". A small piece of our stupidity is the need for approval and the belief that we will get approval if we mirror being normal. There is an ironic element to this thing called approval. It revolves around the nuanced difference between being liked and being respected. To be respected, requires the courage to be disliked.

BANG ON POINT

Don't fool yourself to thinking
that trying to be normal
will be favourable

Bending to the will
and judgment of others
just makes you vulnerable

Normal's just the average
of aberrant after all
a beige median of mediocrity

You're better than that
much better than that
much more better than that
wave goodbye to normal

Everything you say and do
will be scrutinized, judged
and picked to pieces

People will avoid
matters that make 'em think
that's my take

Don't be hazed by their critique
for their failure to see
your way ahead of them
on the bell curve

Be indifferent to them
they tell themselves lies
based on their bias

I would go further and say
that most folk cherry pick
seeing and hearing to respond
and not to understand

Be a kinsman to the weird
scoff at commonness
hang on to that courage

Don't fool yourself to thinking
that trying to be normal
will be favourable

Bending to the will
and judgment of others
'll only make you fuckable

Normal's just the average
of aberrant after all
a beige median of mediocrity

You're better than that
much better than that
much more better than that
wave goodbye to normal

"Everything you say and do will be scrutinised, judged and picked apart. Never delude yourself into thinking that bending to the will and opinions of the people who dislike and disapprove of you will ever cause them to think favourably of you." – Harry Petsanis

I recently watched a Netflix series called *The Waterfront*. Bree, one of the characters witnesses her grandfather's brutal murder. She was a mere child, and while her survival brain caused her to freeze, her thinking brain encoded a myth that she was responsible for his death because she didn't intervene. Her mother forbade Bree from talking about it. Bree ends up assuaging her illusory shame with alcohol and heroin. A subsequent near-death experience results in her spiritual awakening. The adult thinking brain frees the child formally held captive by the survival brain.

BELOW THE WATERLINE

Just above the waterline
the thinking brain
bravely strains
to stay afloat

Down below the waterline
the survival brain
doesn't talk, just bleeds
raw sensation

After major trauma
the survival brain's recall
is frequently
exceedingly corrupted

It may encode bits
thought to be defining
without fitting priming
with no vital validation

You gotta talk
lay bare the myth
share your plight
your body will tell ya
when you get it right

With crippling disquiet
the visceral response
who could deny the need
for something soporific

Who has the insight
to uncover
the real substance
of one's plight

We need
to stay trauma
in the most
efficient way

We need
to keep at bay
whatever lies below
the waterline

You gotta talk
lay bare the myth
share your plight
your body will tell ya
when you get it right

Reference: *Widen the Window*, Elizabeth A. Stanley PhD

Bargara July 2025

I was smitten by snakes from the second I first saw Kaa swimming downstream with Mowgli hanging off his back. Kaa's sheer majesty in the black and white illustrations are forever etched in my imagination. *The Jungle Book* – Rudyard Kipling 1897

KING COBRA

Your appearing stoned me
me, mouth-agape, eyes-agog
dropped my phone on the deck
screen shattered, I winced
your vibe froze my blood
sidewinding n direct
my throat turned dirt dry
I's both roused n nervous
plan B abandoned
heaven only knows why

Tongue hiss your handshake
kill-deal concealed within
treason hid for hell's sake
'tween dying n liven
something soon to begin
my skin broke a shiver
cold-wet beneath this cloak
rifled for my Zippo
lite-n-sucked on a smoke

The circle of life stirs
come-hither chem-scent n more
licking touching n caressing is
squarely what King Cobra's for

With Cobra now at home
'll soon clear the rats n mice
mind, I'll still have a cobra
to keep my heart on ice
WOW, won't that be nice

"A few cobras in your home will soon clear it of rats and mice. Of course, you will still have the cobras."
– Will Cuppy, journalist (1884–1949)

Bargara Sept 2025

To me our antiquated education system and its associated socialisation, bleaches our creative authenticity. Later in life, some of us work hard to try and reclaim it. Pablo Picasso famously said: "Every child is an artist. The problem is how to remain an artist once we grow up." This is my call to arms to circumvent the creativity lost in adulthood.

LEAVE YOUR ADULT AT THE DOOR

When did fun fade
'n life become a chore
why don't we all
wanna play anymore
where did joy go
what happened to awe
why don't we all
wanna dance anymore

Please stop talking for a bit
listen for a lickety-split
when did the child in you
up and disappear
slow down take a breath
stop boring me to death
stop acting so grown-up
restore the kid in there

Be a child again
play wild again
use your genius
delete the reign of adult pain

What are you afraid to lose
when nothing's really yours
enjoy it while you can
as a custodian

why you dress so straight
hit the dress-up box
feel free to be the fool
an unabashed chameleon

Adults are fools
they don't understand
they live in a lala-land
genius is only revealed
when you bend
the rules
adults are fools
who don't understand
they're in flaky chains
genius only thrives
when you bend
the rules

Be a child again
dress wild again
light a fire
and dance
be a child again
act wild again
let your genius
make a
triumphal stand

Inspired by *Genius*, Warren Zevon (released in 2002)

Bargara Dec 2024

For those who don't know, a snollygoster is a shrewd, unprincipled person. Until recently, I did not know that. So when. I was recently challenged to write a poem using "60 English Words You Never Thought Existed" I had a chance to use it. I couldn't use all 60 because that would have been pure ridiculous. I did write this, managing to use 22. Can you pick the words?

SNOLLYGOSTER

What's all
this brouhaha
that's gone 'n' got me
muddled

Some blatherskite's
kerfuffle
gave me cause to
discombobulate

This ragamuffin
threw his taradiddle
bout thingamajigs
n doohickies at me

This gangster
whippersnapper
had me utterly
go giddy

All his
malarkey
was perfectly
designed
to hornswoggle
me

His codswallop
quashed my thinking
obfuscating
any extant inkling

You gotta love
the shenanigans
weaved by
his skulduggery

All his offerings
quite quixotic
do you savvy me
nod if you disagree

Now I'm
just nincompooped
bamboozled by
his ballyhoo

Till finally
by an epiphany
n with serendipity
I did throw
the snollygoster
clear out the window

Dedicated to Danni Stranieri

Note: Defenestration – throwing someone out of a window

Brisbane-Bargara Sept 2025

Attachment Disorder is an expansive clinical term describing disorders of mood, behaviour and social relationships arising from unavailability of normal socialising care and attention from primary caregiving figures in early childhood. It can fuel existentially ruination, or feed creation. I posit, that some folk with it, are driven to take to the stage, and why not.

WATERLINE

On stage
she was free to be
someone other
than the "who" she felt
she was to
her mother

She could hide
her inner child
in plain sight
moving
to the edge
of the spotlight

Hey, I'm okay
I'm fine
just don't look
under the waterline

There's always
two versions of truth
both of 'em wrong
always somethin' else
is goin' on
under the waterline

Outwardly
the swan's gliding
not giving a f**k
inwardly she's fretful
emotionally thrashing
like a duck

Her family scene
had been rough
to her mother
she was never
seen as
good enough

Her mother
passed her own
trauma on
leading to
a hallow-bond
for too long

Hey, I'm okay
I'm fine
just don't look
under the waterline

"The way we talk to our children becomes their inner voice." – Becky Mansfield

Bargara Nov 2024

In 1968, British rock band Cream released a sing titled 'White Room'. The lyrics were composed by poet Pete Brown. This is my homage.

WHITE ROOM

White noise, white space
a hidey-hole from the centre stage
I need a cloud, with silver lining
I'm breaking-out-o-this cougar cage

I want the brouhaha, shut down
I need a little, timeout
in a white room, sunny and warm
just for now, not forever

A white room, w/ white shutters
wide open, to draw de vista in
to see, for miles and miles
and those white horses running wild

I'm looking for, green fields
with maybe, a slow flowing stream
perchance, a little gold
in the sandy river base

This life ain't a party
the critters here, are a hard crowd
there are lions, in this jungle
crouched, and ready to pounce

White room, in a cloud
white noise, not too loud
I do more, when I do nothing
nothin to see here, move on, move on

I wanna break, some R&R
cuz I'm dishevelled, tattered-n-torn
there are lions, in this jungle
crouched, and ready to pounce

White noise, whitespace
I need a break from this ho-hum race
cool fresh air, I must have it
I'm leaving, I'm already gone

White noise, blue-sky horizon
a hidey-hole from the main stage
I need a cloud for preservation
I'm crashing-out-o-this coocoo
coocoo cougar cage

Bargara July 2022

SCIENCE, SICK-OLOGY & MEDICINE

Snappy Cat

Mayhem can feel like a storm that mightily disrupts stability. For some people, it's an unspoken craving; an energy they invite into their lives. These individuals are drawn to drama, and frequent upheaval, because it satisfies a deep-seated psychological and emotional need caused by early childhood trauma.

ADRENALINE

why am I so fond of adrenaline
so besotted by danger's rush
why does my junkie brain
flip logic on its head
n recklessly scorn all that's said

if I did an Inkblot Test
what would it reveal
might further psychometrics
explain how I feel
or the obsessive life I've led

why do I treasure
my twisted view of things
take delight in what provoking you brings
favour rapture over the blasé
inflame others, doin' their heads in

now that my cover's blown
I'll have to own
this craved mayhem
my evil drum
this wicked fun

I hatch antics
invite counter attack
pray you react
try to shoot back
but your bullets are adrenaline
n now it's your bad
you've been had
I win

Most experts say the circumstances in the first 2000 days shape the subconscious brain, and the subconscious brain shape personality.

Bargara Dec 2025

Modern neuroscience views reflective consciousness as a human only adaptation. The early reptilian part of our brain is often forgotten. Yet by volume of neural linkages, the reptilian brain exceeds the 'human' brain 9 to 1. It remains an active emotional warning system that fuels our inner critic.

ASSASSIN

I'm an assassin
every day I kill
a saboteur
who dwells
inside my head
it's my inner critic
if you will

I'm skilled
an old hand
I get the job done
yet he's
always back
the very next day
giving me an earful

Like
the liver
of Prometheus
the saboteur
resurrects
like Jesus
God I'm cross

Taunting me
with questions like
did you think
you'd make it through
without some painful
scratch on you
I'm the boss

The voice says
don't imagine
you'll ever be
the last man standing
I've got dirt on you
there'll be no
soft landing

How 'bout you
have you ever
been at war
inside your head
a battle tale
on the inside
no-one else has read

Once
I nearly
lost it all
I was then
delirious
way too deep in
too sullen to win

I'm an assassin
every day I kill
a saboteur
who dwells
inside my head
my inner critic
if you will

Brisbane March 2025

I demand the right to change my mind whenever I want and without prior notice. That said, I have a hypothesis, based on my lived experience. Perfection exists only in Shangri-La. Perfectionism is a surefire sign of maladaptive attachment early on.

HYPOTHESIS

My supposition is this
in order to exist
we must first survive

For us to survive
we must first be loved
call it as it is,
it's transactional

For us to be loved
we must earn it
by luck or pluck
or sacrifice

By dogged resolution
some will sacrifice their soul
give away their whole
autonomy

By chasing down perfection
we will prove our worth
and its pretence will
belittle us

We will pay the toll
till bankruptcy hits
and we fall to bits
reset and start over

The trials and tribulations
are building blocks
don't seek forgiveness
contrition is for fools

My hypothesis is this
in order to exist
we must fail often and
spectacularly

Toronto Oct 2025

At the age of 72, I think I've earned the right to change my mind whenever I want to and without notice. I've been a swinging voter all my life, but today if the vote was between intoxication and sobriety, I'd vote abstain.

LET'S BE REAL

sedation's overrated
if you need drugs
to have fun
your undoing's
just begun

if you need booze
to help you schmooze
then you're in strife
there's no real pizzazz
in your social life

you shouldn't need
chemicals
to be confident
being straight ain't
an impediment

there's addiction
and there's connection
with a blur in between
which is where
we've all been

that blur's malign
a coping mechanism
this ain't a criticism
just my opinion
our world's got it wrong

there's so many
using something to
help 'em tolerate 'emselves
or placate their fear
of missing out

missing out on what
great question
bravery that's borrowed
joy that's temporary
a freak that's hired

giving you license
to play the fool
to be cool
only you're not
you're just a blunt tool

if you think I'm wrong
please call me out
you can 'ave the high ground
I'm happy in my skin
fine with who I am

I don't need courage
got from a bottle
confidence that's bought
at my brain's expense
I VOTE ABSTAIN

When I pass over, I have requested they play Paul Kelly's song "I've Done All The Dumb Things" as my body is fed into the crematorium's incinerator. I totally own all my faults and misdemeanours. Further, I believe the antecedents were as René Descartes alluded – "The chief cause of human errors is to be found in the prejudices picked up in childhood."

LORE

The stain at my brain's edge was
more 'bout me, than you
you pulled the pin that made me burn
I stayed the course too long

Cuz I'm human I stonewalled
my motherboard fried, my heart froze,

Where to go when the chips are down
how to begin asking why
why pierce my precious shroud like an assassin
then vanish into the crowd

Your bloodless coup made hidden cuts in me
my skin still weeping with woe
ever in awe of that sheath that keeps the hostile out
and me safe within

You breached that border
disturbing the order of all things in me
the welt melted my skin, freeing me to wander in
the universe

Awe will get you through with relish
no longer a stain, now lore

"I function as an asterisk in the limbic system." – S. Kelley Harrell

---

Bargara Oct 2021

Ever since Einstein's quantum physics designated time to be a mere human construct, nothing's lucid to me anymore. Hence, it makes perfect sense that parallel universes do exist. Curiously this replicates the Australian First Nations' mobs belief that they exist alongside those who have passed and those who are yet to be born. This insight shows that 65,000 years ago, they had Albert's smarts.

PARALLEL UNIVERSE

Happens
every other day
one universe pivots
clipping another
and we don't even
feel the nudge
we're totally unaware
of the collision

A leader makes a call
when what's right
isn't on the options list
many blind to the nuance
maybe t'was
a time warped nod
dented from a parallel past
that drew the decision

The dilemma is
people "see"
the resolution
not the courage
or the core uncertainly
we ignore the possibility
this is a time crossing
cosmic chess play

Now I'm sure
parallel universes
often do collide
and more

Life's like chess
the eye's on
the long-game
hoping for a check-mate
knowing that our
five-moves away
future play
will win the day

You must leave
your comfort zone
cuz that's where
the magic happens
sometimes
you gotta dent
your universe
to recreate yourself

Sometimes
there's an edge
attached to being bold
even mindfully reckless
take into account
that parallel universes
do collide
and often

Now I'm sure
parallel universes
often do collide
and more

"We're here to put a dent in the universe." - Steve Jobs (1955-2011)

Brisbane Feb 2025

I recently attended a doctors-only selfcare retreat. For a practicing physician, it reiterated what I always hear on aircraft. When the sky falls in, always place the oxygen mask on yourself first, then you will be capable of caring for others. Self-care isn't selfish, it's an imperative.

PLATO'S CAVE[1]

Connection
must be passionate
for passionate connection's
time well spent

Inside Plato's Cave
there're just shadows
turnabout, walk out
take in the outside air

It's a sore truth
that busy isn't busy
creativity's the fruit
of a still mind

Step away
from the hustle
and the bustle
embrace a silent space

A garden
a forest
or a place
by the sea

Still gently
push beyond
the window
of tolerance

Your best ideas
will often come
from the
ablution suite

Make sure
you log them
on your
timesheet

Discount
the cost of chaos
we're
not broken

Curiosity's
my superpower
for me it means
self-mastery

Never a "should"
rather a "need"
I notice
without judgement

There's nothing
woo-woo here
Plato's Cave will make
you a slave

1. Plato's famous parable about the prisoners who mistake shadows for reality.

Bowral, NSW May 2025

Don't misunderstand me. I'm not having a go at teachers. Most teachers are excellent. I was unsettled by resent research suggesting that teachers who spoke too fast were 40% more likely to refer their students for an assessment of a potential neurodivergent diagnosis. Are special skills teachers remediating 'poor' students or 'poor' teachers.

SEA OF BLAH

Please slow down
you talk too fast
drowning us
in a sea of blah

We're tortured by
your jagged babble
you're the problem here
you're the trouble

Your teaching's twisted
like a corkscrew ride
can't you see
we're torn inside

Those hairpin turns
just produce
a fight or flight hit
they're of no use

We want to learn
your wheels are spinning
but you're not winning
our hearts

Our failings aren't
due to our neglect
and with respect
nor our defiance

So don't refer us on
for our behaviour
when it's really
your failure

Maybe you
oughta
go back to school
and learn more about us

Let's change the sea of blah
to a sea of ah-ha
we all see it now
let's start over again

We want to learn
your wheels are spinning
but you're not winning
our hearts

'Another Brick in the Wall' – Pink Floyd

Kiama May 2025

My side-hustle is as an Addiction Medicine Physician in the public sector. Some call this the Deep End of healthcare. After twenty five years in this field, I've come to the conclusion that I don't treat addiction at all. Without exception, drugs were the solution to a world rife with Adverse Childhood Events suffered by sensitive kids. Drugs worked perfectly well until they didn't. Can we please stop or at least dial down the stigma.

SENSITIVE MINDS

To him
a touch was a blow
each word a roar
realness misery
blackouts
ecstasy

To her
a random
was a confidant
each wooer a lover
each lover
her next best God

For them
failing was usual
every affray
a calming thing
delinquency wicked
so let wicked begin

To them
skip-bins were a shelter
nowhere more like home
any pill the answer
injected even better
begot by a burner phone

They say
I'd never get it
wouldn't even wanna
share
their idea
of nirvana

I hear 'em
from my privileged space
I'm the enemy
to them I mirror
their childhood
tormentors

Encircled
by pariahs
drugs plugged a hole
in their souls
made 'em feel
safe for a while

For them
to feel alive
they had
an exit plan
call the man
on a burner phone

Bargara Nov 2024

The term "monkey chatter" comes from Zen Buddhism. It refers to the silent monologue that passes, mostly negative, judgment on an individual's every action, thought, and perceived misstep. When really bad, the monkeys can drive a sane person to drugs and drink.

SHAMAN'S POV

From a shaman's
point of view
we are all still
tied down to
tiny shards of us
scattered n locked
up in our past

That crap-rage is
hex energy in motion
a max heady
love potion
setting feelings
firing throughout
our minds n bodies

When those feelings
r real 'bad'
it's maybe cuz we had
a dose of
shame and guilt
driven
dis-ease

Finally we
laid our dirty
secrets out
n suddenly
our f#?k-monkeys
became our saviours

We became
more forgiving
of ourselves
a more
tolerant world
could have saved
a zillion lives

For the first
time ever
we were cut down
never felt so high
in our lives
our bingo cards
were called

Have you ever
felt anything
like this
before
I know you to
will get through
fact is I'm sure of it

Cairns Oct 2025

In her 2003 essay 'The Spoon Theory', Christine Miserandino describes her experience with chronic illness using a handful of spoons as a metaphor for units of finite energy available to perform her daily functions. The metaphor has since been used to describe a wide range of disabilities, including neurodiversity, that might place unseen burdens on individuals. I think it's about giving ourselves permission to sometimes "call it a day" early.

SIX SPOON DAY

To begin
I's already
two spoons in
hey
it's just a
six spoon day

Halfway in
I's four
spoons down
n I'm still going
yeah, think I'll
get there

For a bit
I's raw
dogging it
hey
it's just a
six spoon day

I treat myself
like a disease
I'm not
always at ease
but I'm
at peace now

I chucked it in
not gonna
make it
through today
hey it's just a
six spoon day

Yes I
chucked it in
n that's okay
I'm saving
myself for
another day

Many people think that eating sugar will give you a sudden 'sugar hit' or a burst of energy. This belief is more myth than reality. Modern neuroscience has shown that eating sugar does not make children hyperactive, despite some parents' perception that it does. The hit may have less to do with blood sugar and more to do with the fact that sugar causes the brain to release dopamine and endogenous opioids, chemicals that give you a feeling of pleasure. The jolt of energy is likely from the same chemicals released with other addictive triggers (like alcohol or cocaine) and creating cravings for more. Thanks to neuroscience, another myth is unravelling.

SUGAR HIT

Mum I need
a sugar hit
a spoonful to zip
me up a bit

I felt an twitch
and now
I have to
follow it

If you're tracking
my persuasion
I just need
to fly

I don't wanna
stand in line
I want it now
I don't have time

I need
speedy satisfaction
I won't repeat it
now means now

Warm candles
caught my eye
can't explain it
don't know why

It set me on
this campaign
I need a sugar hit
I won't ask you again

This may seem
like a random thing
but it's a thing
nevertheless

My beige life
has no hard edges
my edges
are all tacky

I need
a sugar hit
a metaphor for
I want more

"Brown sugar, how come you taste so good?" – Mick Jagger & Keith Richards, 1969

Many years ago, when I was an emergency physician and department head, the ambulance delivered a gentleman in his late sixties with a history of schizophrenia, who had poured an accelerant over his naked body and set himself alight. He had over 80% burns, mostly full thickness. I rang the tertiary burns unit boss, a friend of mine and he suggested terminal sedation, as the degree of his injury was nonsurvivable. For those unaware, this is an ambiguous zone. Euthanasia is illegal but managing suffering is ethically legitimate. The term terminal sedation is commonly used in palliative care, when the delivery of drugs designed to manage suffering carry an inevitable consequence.

THIS IS GONNA HURT

Beware
this is gonna hurt
you'll cry
a natural response
here's why

Each death
will take you back
to that grim place
where your first loss
was darker than black

Each time
you cry
your tears show
that you're vulnerable
you're human

Death asked life
how come everyone
loves you
but fears me
life replied
cuz I'm the beautiful lie
and you're
the painful truth

Compassion
comes at a cost
calling for
all concerned
to hurt together

The first time
then each next time
is fraught
with the thought
that we will all die

Here's the rub
my vulnerability
my authenticity
is not yours to take
only mine to give

Death upsets me
still I took the syringe
and gave terminal sedation
whilst I gazed compassionately
into his grateful eyes
Then my team all stood
held each other's hands
and whispered RIP

Compassion = to suffer together

Sentosa, Singapore Jan 2025

Jung warned if we don't consciously evolve, we unconsciously decay. "Without inner reflection, your psyche becomes like an untended garden overgrown with fears, outdated beliefs, and unconscious habits that quietly choke your potential".[1]

WELCOME BACK (TO SOMEONE THAT I USED TO KNOW)

Ruination came silently, nothing too sudden, souring surreptitiously
in slow-mo and unannounced; awakening exhausted, sleep unrestorative
feeling strangely muddled, with less to give; reason crumbled
connections frayed, wheels spun; slow decaying had begun

I gradually became aware I wasn't going anywhere; despair started
dripping in, what was my sin; couldn't fathom why patterns kept repeating
I began to cry, there'd been no warning, hidden forces foiled my inner world
until I couldn't recognise myself

The "someone" that I denied, ended up controlling me
the fragments I'd repressed and were not addressed never disappeared
now disguised as addictions inflicting brain pain

"Who me, ever gets angry"; no, me, Zen master – bullshit; self-harm
repressed rage that could at any stage have me hit out; my dark traits
were only dangerous coz I dismissed them; disallowing them to exist
whatever I repressed became a burden until expressed
in the end it will come out as a god almighty guttural shout

Finally I did burnout, following a trail of self-betrayal; meaninglessness
made my psyche collapses; I was spiritually parched from a lack of purpose
sure, there was trauma in my past relationships, but those ships have sailed
they don't prevail anymore; I won't let the past narrate or recreate
a mission without your permission

I will step into conflicts way anytime, any day, only if that's my decision
but I won't become emotional and cause dumb derision
if emotions are required then so be it; I will not lie to myself
there's no big deal wishing my shadow-self to heal

1. Jung Warned Us: The 7 Hidden Forces That Quietly Destroy Your Inner Life,
Isabella – Medium: Read and Write Stories (Dec 5, 2025)

Hamilton Island Dec 2025

I concede that understanding sometimes requires deconstruction. It therefore makes sense that we create separate disciplines. Ultimately these disciplines should be reconstructed for the purpose of creating true knowledge as all knowledge is connected. Paradoxically, the person with doubt is often more informed than the know-all. Boxes limit our view.

WHAT BOX

There's grace in making
a poem, a melody
putting together
pieces of history
creating a fresh view
of our past

There's splendour in taking
pure maths and creating
a brand new equation
like energy equals mass
multiplied by
the speed of light squared

There's maths in music
artifice in a crystal
lies in philosophy
truth in fiction
and politics
in religion

You say
think outside
the box
I say
what box
please explain

Your attempt
to box things
into disciplines
seems incorrect
in the face of the unity
of all knowledge

The analyst, scientist
the economist, poet
the artisan, musician
all have one thing
in common
they are curious

There's maths in music
artifice in a crystal
lies in philosophy
truths in fiction
and politics
in religion

You say
think outside the box
I say what box
don't restrain
bring back the polymath
again

"All literate men are sustained by the philosopher, the historian, the political analyst, the economist, the scientist, the poet, the artisan, and the musician." – Glenn T. Seaborg (1912-1999)

Shanghai April 2025

Compelling evidence indicates that the First 2000 Days from conception, profoundly shape our lives. The argument goes: environment shapes our subconscious, and our subconscious shapes our personality. As a philosophical dilettante, I'm drawn to the Chinese curse: "May you live in interesting times." The expression is ironic as 'interesting' times means troubled. Our existence happens at life-speed. Collisions are frequent, unavoidable, and they wound us. These wounds are subliminal and thus invisible. They're inflicted in the space where our core values, emotions and passions reside.

WOUNDS OF EXISTENCE
[THEY MAKE OR BREAK US]

I'm meeting with my inner child
it's his sapience I'm after
keen to know his lore
his whyfor
he whispers he wished he'd lived
in more "interesting" times
interesting his byword
for much more troubled
meanwhile I'm heeding
the sound of ceiling fan blades
sectioning air whilst I'm
nestled in a wicker chair
a cotton kapok cushion
between me and the cane
cancels out any chance
of corrugated buttock pain
I'm snared by the scent
from frangipani flowers
wafting thru the louvers
in the early evening hours
I listen with curiosity
as he conveys with finesse
why we can't address what we
can't access in our subconscious

Hail to existence
but fuck the dissonance
tween the past and what
might yet come to pass
it's our psyche talking
our inner thoughts stalking
ruining our connection
to the here and now
our idiot brain
is purposely designed
to persistently aggravate
our wounds of existence
I have more questions
than I have answers
but there's no angst in me
cuz I simply adore irony
I have an aha moment
triggered by the floral scent
wafting thru the louvers
we're all our own muses
now aint that amusing
praise the paradox
and the irony of
our wounds of existence

"The most potent muse of all is our own inner child." - Stephen Nachmanovitch (né 1950)

MORALITY, STRUGGLE, GOD and CONFLICT

Neilsen Park KN

I am grateful to live in Australia. We have a peaceful democracy. When elections are held, the transition is dignified. The fact that elsewhere, mankind continues to wage war, astounds me. When will we all ever learn to be peaceful warriors.

APES OF WAR

The sky may explode
best shield your eyes
you'll wanna squeal
cover up your mouth
it could get loud
so cup your ears

See no evil
speak no evil
hear no evil
still there will
be tears

Carthaginian Peace
is what they'll seek
settlement based on
breaking us
making us weak

The harshest
of terms
will be imposed
we'll won't capitulate
we'll be repressed
everyone knows

We'll rise up
never be defeated
we'll fight on
after all
there's nothing
to lose

we're not
ordinary apes
we're ace predators
we're apes
of war

The sky may explode
best shield your eyes
you'll wanna squeal
cover up your mouth
it could get loud
so cup your ears

See no evil
speak no evil
hear no evil
still there will
be tears

Former Methodist minister, William Booth, along with his wife, Catherine, founded The Salvation Army in the slums of London during 1865. William wanted to make the church more accessible to the whole community at a time when many poor and working class people were excluded from churches. Since it was founded in 1865 The Salvation Army has been opposed to the use of alcohol.

BLOOD AND FIRE

Said his dad
was a Sally Man
untutored to that term
I asked Michael
to please explain

they're preachers
of a kind he said
bearing an army zeal
and brass band music
to add to their appeal

"Blood and Fire"
was their shtick
taken straight from the script
as written in the Book
of the Apocalypse

The Sallys
took their ministry
from the church
and directly
into struggle street

After all
church is a holy place
embellished with riches
somewhere for the gentry
to obtain grace

The Sallys focus
was those in real need
those in privation
either body or soul
those truly needing salvation

The Sally Men waged war
declared by a Rogue Rev
on a mission
to ease human suffering
they preached prohibition

No more alcohol
Cuz booze
stole your soul
the only true spirit
was the spirit of faith

Religion's always fine
till corporatised
and real estate
becomes their
central dictate

Mike and I smiled
finished up our wine
our souls in a good place
we felt fine
no "Blood and Fire" here

Bargara Nov 2024

The Human Genome Project (1990-2003) demonstrated 99.9% DNA concordance between all humans. Thus, difference accounts for 0.1 %. It follows that diversity, equity, and inclusion should be nonissues. Yet privilege begets privilege begets entitlement. Until the privileged need an organ transplant. Then, any human organ will do. How ironic. BTW - Bogan is Australian and New Zealand slang for a person whose speech, clothing, attitude and behaviour are considered unrefined or unsophisticated. They've done poorly in the lottery of life.

BOGAN LINE

We are all sinners
we're all gonna die
there'll be no winners
north of the Bogan Line

We're all doomed to fail
in the same way as a fish
who can't climb a tree
just the privileged will prevail

Round here fairness is
impossible to find
eyes are useless
when the mind is blind

Diversity don't exist
Equity, what's that
inclusion's an illusion
all of this is fact

Although we're all
plainly the same
the privileged play
the "difference" game

When we die
they'll want your heart
but please note
you'll also get my mother
she might wanna haunt you
north of the Bogan Line

We are all sinners
we're all gonna die
there'll be no winners
north of the Bogan Line
my mother
might wanna haunt you
from north of the Bogan Line

"The eyes are useless when the mind is blind." - Mark Venturini

Basel August 2024

I recently attended a scientific addiction medicine conference in Montréal, Canada. The keynote, Courtland Warren, was outstanding. He proposed that addiction is reaching for something that is known and therefore safe, because of the need to assuage a deep sense of not being good enough. Ultimately if we don't move forward it's because we feel we don't deserve to move forward. So we have to do some compassion work in order to change our self-identity. Our minds are the medicines that can change our identity.

CREEP

We're all creeps
needing to cross the street
n face certain danger
like rapping with a stranger

Our crooked moral compass
runs on avoidance
n the fear of leaving
a safe place

We're not seduced
by the pain
of having to adjust n
start over again

Sometimes life is
difficult to watch
and harder
to live through

Addiction's a pattern
you can't escape
despite the fact
it comes with a cost

We're all somehow addicted
to playing
in an unfair yet
familiar place

Resilience
they say 's
the only way
to transform yourself

Never take nothing
personally
control it's spread
n move on

Adversity's
something
happening for me
n not something agin

Remember this
our minds
r the best
medicine

Safety is the status quo
growth is dangerous
freedom's on the other side
of life's resistance

Am I enough
I am capable
I am deserving
f$&k yeah I sure am

"Between stimulus and response there is a space. In that space is our power to choose our response. In our response lies our growth and our freedom." – Viktor E. Frankl

Montréal Oct, 2025

In his play The Tempest, William Shakespeare famously wrote, "Hell is empty and all the devils are here." Devils prey on the young and vulnerable. Those previously targeted, recognise those newly preyed upon and can provide priceless solace and a way forward. Life's individual trauma collapses when shared. Meanwhile, between spiteful strikes, devils tap their fingers on the tabletop, whilst planning their next skirmish. Be prepared.

DEVIL'S TATTOO*

I saw the look
in your eyes
a look I knew
all too well

That look
took me back
to when I'd lived
in your hell

When my life
held your pain
dealt out by
a heinous guy

The devil had
me stay *shtum*
now I
understood why
the fiend's
finger's
had tapped
the devil's tattoo anew

In your eyes
I saw
Season Two
unfold

I saw
your survival brain
being hacked
no turning back

They say
it takes a village
to raise
a child
the child
not loved will
burn the village down
just to feel warm

Regret
ain't seen it yet
still the devil
keeps tapping

"It takes a village to raise a child.
The child who is not embraced by the village will burn it down to feel its warmth."
A proverb that exists in many different African languages.

* The Devil's Tattoo refers to rhythmic finger tapping, simulating a military drum beat.

Canberra June 2025

'All You Need Is Love' is a song written by John Lennon in 1967 and credited to Lennon-McCartney. I prefer to imagine that no one truly writes lyrics or poems. Rather, they hold up their hands to the cosmos and catch what is percolating up there at any moment in time. With that in mind, I suspect that Lennon was tapping into thoughts that Albert Camus had earlier caught.

DUTY AND LOVE

Albert Camus
pulled through a war
God knows what he saw
Was it war that bore
his lore of the absurd

He once wrote
if he had to write a book
on morality it would be
one hundred pages long
and ninety-nine would be blank.

On the final page
he would write
I recognise
only one duty
and that is to love

But what is love
of course
Camus had
his own view
to argue

He said love
like art and beauty
is an act of rebellion
against
a meaningless world

Love is a way
of facing sure death
and suffering
without surrendering
to despair

Fell those inner thoughts
that foster indecision
choose to live with passion
even when success
isn't guaranteed

As in The Myth
of Sisyphus
stand stronger than the rocks
we're decreed to carry
and do so with glee

Love is neither naïve nor safe
create your own meaning
lean in with fervour
refuse to be broken
by the certainty of death

On the final page
he would write
I recognise
only one duty
and that is to love.

'Absurdity may be king, but love saves us from it.' – Albert Camus

Reference: https://iai.tv/articles/albert-camus-on-love-and-the-absurd-auid-1317

Kiama May 2025

Self-talk occurs in several ways. The Dialogical Self Theory assumes lots of inner voices. Internal dialogical activity implies an exchange of thoughts or ideas between at least two inner-selves representing specific points of view. Among the reason for self-talk are self-criticism, self-reinforcement.* I have an inner troll and an inner sage who just love a raucous debate.

FLASH & MITCH

my inner troll
versed my inner sage
Flash versus Mitch
can't recall which one's which

their bickering is bitter
all for its own sake
keeps me awake
damn, what a bitch

due to my naivety
they pull the rug from under me
please help me
flick the off switch

will I take a Valium
maybe drink some wine
sit cross-legged and meditate
each would be fine

or I could grab a pen
n journal how I feel
move the words around a bit
make the lyrics real
play some chords, n sing it

now, I'm standing here
guitar in hand
the choice clear
I think, I'm Mitch

*Ref: Oleś PK, Brinthaupt TM, Dier R and Polak D (2020) Types of Inner Dialogues and Functions of Self-Talk: Comparisons and Implications. *Front. Psychol.* 11:227. doi: 10.3389/fpsyg.2020.00227

A friend sent me a link to Munk Debate on Political Correctness (PC). For PC is stifling the free and open debate that fuels our democracy. Stephen Fry was as always erudite arguing that PC has gone too far. I couldn't help thinking that Donald Trump may be doing us all a favour by trashing PC in almost every media appearance he makes. Ironically, there may be some merit in Trump after all.

FLIP THE SWITCH ON PC

The best thing
that Trump's done
is thumb his nose
at PC

The total bore
that DT is
he won't bow
to the PC biz

PC distorts
useful debate
and creates
tailored woke

Of course I want
all of us
to treat each other
well

The question is
how do
we reach this
dire groundswell

PC
hasn't managed to
do as intended
banish bigotry

F#&k
the preacher's
prudish
pulpit talk

It's vague
and abstruse
misdirected
not of much use

It's like walking
on eggshells
it's a crafted
coverup

Be a contrarian
fault is fine
angels fly cuz
they take 'emselves lightly

PC has
turned into a joke
it's now a yoke
stifling conversation

Let's engage
in doubt
tell our truths as they are
PC's gone too far

Bargara July 2025

When Napoleon Bonaparte was criticised for winning battles simply because of luck, he famously retorted: "I'd rather have lucky generals than good ones." More than a hundred years later, Eisenhower reaffirmed this point by saying: "I'd rather have a lucky general than a smart general. They win battles." The ironic thing about leadership roles is that successful leaders rely on relationships with their subordinates, as much as luck. Indeed it has been implied that if you need to use the power inherent in your position, then you never really had it. Leaders who have distain for their "followers" and thus micromanage, are doomed. Real power and leadership is built on human connection, respect and trust. This General, the subject of my poem is in my opinion way too concrete.

GENERAL

Deer in headlights
stiff with fear
unable to blink
let alone think

Like I'm atta gathering
and they can't separate
dumb from genius
makes me furious

Deer in headlights
stiff with fear
unable to blink
let alone think

Hell there's
group think
opinions, ignorance
then there's what I think

Please God
make a medicine
for everyone else to take
so all will agree with me
make me the General

In a land of fools
stupidity's insidious
there's a clear cry
for someone imperious
why can't they just
follow me

I am the General
I am amenable
to steer the deer
in headlights
stiff with fear
unable to blink
let alone... please God
make a medicine
for everyone else to take
so all will agree with me
make me the General

Please God
make a medicine
for everyone else to take
so all will agree with me
make me the General

Bargara Feb 2024

There seems to be a lot of 'misplaced' sense of entitlement in certain quarters. The irony and paradox are not lost on me.

HEY SIR

Hey Sir, I find it funny
that you're banking on a win
so, what have you done
to expect such a thing

Heard you wanna fruitful life
maybe even live forever
tell me who're you to land that fate
hey, laugh out loud whatever

I heard once you broke down
at one point you never slept
held you head in your hands
and wept – you were
a sodden mess

Hey Sir, have a nice day
I wish that you have a nice life
still I'm not quite clear
as to what's driving you my dear

Eleanor-outlaw gladly
tanked and threw a match
then making good she dowsed it
again, another wet patch

Sounds like, ya didn't win after all
hey mister, that's not funny
who were you to want to score
when it's just 'bout the journey
and then no more

"Water, water everywhere, nor any drop to drink."
- Samuel Taylor Coleridge, *The Rime of the Ancient Mariner*

Bargara Sept 2022

I work with people who've had Adverse Childhood Events, which has handcuffed them to an injurious 'here'. It's a 'here' that we try to help them escape. At times we can, at other times we can't.

HORSEMAN

Must be some kinda way outta here, but I'm not gunning for that, hear me
cuz outta here's just another stop, what I crave is a journey
must be some kinda way outta here

I've been tethered for far too long, the hankering to stay here's been strong
halting my need to grow, leaving me unable to move on
must be some kinda way outta here

I wanna be a horseman in cadence with my steed, in tune with my mount's trot

I've been stagnant for far too long, but now being still fills me with dread
I need to grow by moving on, "here" is just another word for braindead
must be some kinda way outta here

I wanna be a horseman in cadence with my steed, in tune with my mount's trot
my steed's strut will take me on a journey, which I know will help a lot

There's power in movement, there's panache in not standing still
stayed to a burning platform, designed to silently kill
must be some kinda way outta here
but I'm not looking for more mazy strife
I don't wanna swap "here" for the next dead-end stop
I'm looking to a spirited journey of life

I wanna be a horseman in cadence with my steed, in tune with my mount's trot
my steed's strut will take me on a journey which I know
must be some kinda way outta here, must be some kinda way outta here
must be some kinda way outta here, must be

Partially inspired by 'All Along The Watchtower', Bob Dylan

Docklands, Melbourne October 2024

I believe religion is useful for many, in that it provides fellowship and succour. I believe I've been blessed personally, by having a crack crew of guardian angels looking over me, although I don't have enough mental gigabytes to know who they answer to. My church is the beach, my hymns are anything music. All on earth, past present and emerging, are my siblings.

I Have More Questions Than I Have Answers

Jew by chance
Muslim by accident
Christian by fate
all decided
by a throw
of the dice

Hindu by issue
Buddhist by karma
Shinto by fluke
all well beyond
our own
device

You speak Spanish
I speak English
You speak Cantonese
funny how
none of us
ever got
to choose

I love masculine
I love feminine
I love anything
that doesn't
make me feel
I'm being screwed

What's this thing
called congregation
why do we seek
to divide and conquer
why can't we be humble
and meek enough
to concur

The folly
the paradox
presence of irony
the powerplay
by an elite few
truly stupefies me

"What religion a man shall have is a historical accident, quite as much as what language he shall speak."
– George Santayana, philosopher (1863–1952)

Bargara Dec 2024

One of my favourite things, is talking shit with random strangers. Before you get confused, when I say shit, I mean good shit, an Australian idiom. Recently my wife and I dined with a group that included Zaneta, a glaciologist from the Czech Republic. Her personality was magnetic. In her spell, I pledged to write a poem. This is it. Now I'm looking for a metal band to make the words explode into song.

ICE QUEEN

In a land
of myth and maybe
I warmed to
an Ice Queen

We dined off
and on each other
both of us
keen

Me a man
she mostly reptile
the Ice Queen
tickled my spirit
with her tongue
it slithered deep
inside my soul
seemed to me
we got along

I'd forgotten
my blood was fire
her's was ice, she chilled
me to the very bone

Was this her plan
all along
wrought by
her reptile brain

At first her tickling
was enticing
icicles formed in me

Ice crystals like diamonds
made me sparkle
I brushed aside the sirens
she was a drug

Reptiles kill
when they sense danger
my sole want
was to be a friend
I wrote this song
to ask you
how did we
get it so wrong
yes, what went wrong

Was her pretence
to "entertain"
meant for
herself alone
just a ruse
wrought by
her reptile brain
so had I
been duped again

Dedicated to Zaneta – glaciologist and tour guide, Scenic Tour Greenland Iceland

In 1990, Kev Carmody and Paul Kelly penned the song 'From Little Things Big Things Grow'. Fittingly, in writing that song they 'paid homage' to Springsteen, Dylan, Guthrie and others, who iteratively stole 'bits' from others before them. Such is the irony of creativity.

IRONY

Size ain't important
nothing's too small
everything's something
crucial after all

The tiniest detail
could be a sign
of somethin' bigger
coming down the line

Those tiny bright lights
may flag a safe place to land
or umpteen crab eyes
at night in the sand

Irony's whit is
the twist in the game
a banter, a satire
hooking our attention
challenging our schema

the bigger the billboard
the larger the lie
the louder the scream
the softer the sigh

A pinprick can kill
as fast as a hammer
thinking back, Cupid's arrow
could stop u in your tracks

Don't sweat the small stuff
is a common pitch
as is the adage if you count
your pennies you'll be rich

Hey, the reason we often
find ourselves in
difficult places always begins
by being too blasé

Irony's whit is
the twist in the game
a banter, a satire
hooking our attention
challenging our schema

Sizing up happens
in our mind
based on assumptions
embalmed in flaws

Size isn't important
nothing's too small
everything's something
crucial after all

The tiniest detail
could be a sign
of somethin bigger
down the line

Steal Like An Artist, Austin Kleon, published in 2012, Workman Publishing

Bargara April 2025

I recently watched the TV series *Mindhunter*. The premise was that to catch a serial killer requires exploring the villain's mind and studying how they think. The assertion being that their monstrous proclivity was the product of a damaged psyche, a result of nurture rather than nature. But, what if in their minds, their criminal acts were the only thing that makes them truly feel alive. Having been themselves denied the sanctity of life, they have a contrary view of its worth.

MINDHUNTER

Inside
everyone
lies a who
yet names
are but labels
without meaning

Please pay close attention as I
choose my words with care
there'll be no repetition

The where
right now's
irrelevant
as we're all
in a prison cell
a place of our own making

Please pay close attention as I
choose my words with care
there'll be no repetition

The what
the purpose
is simple
I plan to thrive
I need to feel ablase
to be afire to survive

Come walk with me
come talk to me
'bout how an' why we don't share
the same view of probity

The when
is soon
as you'll understand
I'm in a rush to get my
erotic contraband

Please pay close attention as I
choose my words with care
there'll be no repetition

As for
the why
that's simple
it's cuz I am entitled
and cuz I can

The how
is best described
by saying
therein lies
the rub
as the bard would tell us
Come walk with me...

"To catch a criminal, you have to think like one." - Stephen King

I presently accept as an article of faith, that the truth is unknowable. This is due in part to my hunch, that we unknowingly filter only what our senses reveal. I guess that makes me a fan of Carl Jung who said *"I was driven to ask myself in all seriousness: 'What is the myth you are living?' ... So, I took it upon myself to get to know 'my' myth, and I regarded this as the task of tasks..."*
This poem seeks to put that abstract notion onto a canvas, in words.

NO SHIT SHERLOCK

We only see
who we want to be
our mind's designed
for the shallow

Like how
I know you
better than I know
myself

Each time
I check the mirror
I wholly
make myself up

I run
to the dress-up box
and let the witches
dress me

The seers
know how
to lose
a chaperone

I run
a red light
and crash into
this state of affairs
no shit Sherlock

Make the puzzle
a curio
who cares
who's really there

To shift
what you see
you gotta switch
how you think

A hustler
knows
to spy you gotta hide
in the open

lean t'wards
black numbers
on the roulette wheel
then spin the spiel

To find
what's real
you gotta play
on a wider stage

Share your vision
with the right crew
I hope
you find 'em
no shit Sherlock

"Having eyes, do you not see? And having ears, do you not hear? And do you not remember?"
- Mark 8:18, Literal standard version

Bargara May 2024

When you see injustice, don't look away, because silence helps the perpetrators. Be bold and hold firm. P.S. Most police officers behave with the highest integrity.

NOT UNTOUCHABLE

Wallace was of colour
Queen of Sheba-esque
her august posture cautioning
don't mess with me

Her silence bore witness
to her ever mindfulness
always calm and poised
even in distress

Mercer was a cocky cop
a whitey on a power trip
hiding behind a badge
he thought he was untouchable

He had still to learn
Wallace outmatched him
in every worldly way
that truly matters

She was driving late at night
through empty streets
in a black SUV, nothing fancy
clean, simple, quiet like Wallace

She was humming softly
to the sound of the tires
on the road, her mind
was already home

Mercer saw a chance
to make his night
after all he was bored
and keen to show his might

Fifteen years on the force
he'd earned a seedy reputation
he had his arrogance to feed
on the road he was the law

Mercer wrote out a ticket
blatantly a sham
her jaw tightened, she stayed calm
resolved to foil this small man

Wallace had no time
for petty fights
but this fight was for those
of colour, forced to cower

She filed a civil rights complaint
for his abuse of power
unlawful detainment
and tried intimidation

The jury found in favour of Wallace
on the night in question
Mercer didn't see
Wallace as a person

Reference: He Thought His Badge Made Him Untouchable – Until He Brought the Wrong Woman to Court, 29 March 2025

Bargara July 2025

I recently had the pleasure of seeing *O, Ophelia*. It was written and directed by Amber Grossmann, the founder of an emerging youth theatre company Overall Arts. It was a modern tale of codependent relationships exploring themes of coercive control and emotional abuse in young relationships, and at the same time exploring the role of Ophelia, the tragic heroine in Shakespeare's *Hamlet*. It prompted me to write this poem.

OPHELIA – I FEEL YA

I stand tall
I have liberty
I carry no tragedy
I've won the lottery

I stand straight
with no naiveté
no innate coercion
bothers me, anymore

No watery abyss
will drown me
I swim free
and comfortably

Chaos brought
on by others
washes over me
I'm no one's pawn

I have agency
identity
I have prospects
for the future

It wasn't always so
in a past life
I existed solely
to advance the sick story
of an abusive other
like Hamlet and Ophelia

Yes
there was sex
in her violence
she a lioness, me a lamb

It's a well
trodden tale
I was expendable
a male Ophelia

She was Hamlet
I her marionette
hard bitten
forbidden fruit

Fool me once
shame on you
fool me twice
shame on me

I'll not be
a victim twice
understand this
what you did
was nothing nice

Now
I have agency
and prospects
for the future
I'm no Ophelia

Albert Camus wrote *L'Étranger* in 1942 (translated as *The Stranger* or *The Outsider* in English). Seen as a classic of 20th-century literature, *L'Étranger* received critical acclaim for Camus's absurd existentialist view. Like all great writing, it is open to interpretation. In 1977 it served me well by ending my "brief obsessive desire" to end my life. I came to understand that absurdly, existential crises were essential for personal growth. Serenity requires gratitude, which in turn requires accepting the "gentle indifference of the world." This poem is my take on the central themes of Camus's novella.

OUTSIDER

The courtroom
the crucifix
the sun and the sea
were the death of me

The courtroom
was the court of society
its fiction meant that I
could never be free

The crucifix
set fixed beliefs
ruling on how and
how not to be

I was an outsider
to this order
I was indifferent
to the crucifix

The sun beamed
oppressive heat
a slap in the face
only the sea
gave me relief
that and time
I spent with Marie

Here's the question
was I misunderstood
or did I understand
the folly of man

Indifference
to mainstream
convention
can be lethal

The crux of life
is quite blurred
trying to find meaning
was to me absurd

I am a
stranger
detached from life
and thus spurred
by the court
the sun and
the crucifix

Did I
die for truth
or die defying
the crudity of life

Was I a Christ
or an Antichrist
a secular Jesus
or a raw sensualist

Here's the question
was I misunderstood
or did I understand
the folly of man

Bargara April 2025

Life is concrete and laid-back for the lucky few. However, most of us carry an unconscious moral wound and need a regular brain defrag or a software upgrade. Psychologists call this reframing our quirky reckoned reality. Most humans are born with real and/or imagined trauma, which is amplified by our Idiot Brain. Defrag is the process of existential rehabilitation. Trauma is incessant until we make peace with our 'Shadow Self' (C Jung). Until then we're condemned to live in a rehab we can't escape – aka 'Hotel California' (The Eagles).

PANTOUM – REHAB THAT NEVER ENDS

It happened six-days in
I was joined in the pool by a young girl
the creepy-crawly was annoying me
before she dived in, she pulled the creepy-crawly out

I was joined in the pool by a young girl
I remember her whenever I hit a snag
before she dived in, she pulled the creepy-crawly out
today I hit a snag

I remember that young girl whenever I hit a snag
I recall that day back then
that morning I again hit a snag
often I ask why I must relearn the same thing each day

I daily relive that day back then
when the creepy-crawly annoyed me
often I ask why I must relearn the same thing each day
it happened six-days in

"Sometimes we don't want to heal because the pain is the last link to what we have lost." – Ibn Sina

Melbourn Nov 2025

I'm beginning to wonder if watching TV news is hindering my mental wellbeing. Man is the apex predictor. Israel versus Palestine. Russia versus Ukraine. Then there's the many untold conflict stories in Africa. Even the United States of America is anything but united. It seems that the human construct of patriotism is a massive con.

PATRIOTISM

Patriotism is
combustible trash
ready to be torched
by those with ambition

Patriotism can
be matched to the fact
that it's the last refuge
of the patrician

Grab a match
strike it
let's incinerate
all sensible debate

History is polished
honed to perfection
so as to reflect
feats of the great

With all due respect to
history's enlightened
it's sour when written
by a blind wordsmith

"Patriotism, n. Combustible rubbish ready to the torch of anyone ambitious to illuminate his name. In Dr Johnson's famous dictionary patriotism is defined as the last refuge of a scoundrel. With all due respect to an enlightened but inferior lexicographer I beg to submit it is the first." – Ambrose Bierce (1842–1914)

Bargara August 2025

I often reflect on the old refrain, "war, what is it all for". Obviously, the privileged few get a "sugar hit" out of it; a placebo effect to make up for the injurious childhood events they suffered. Why do they inflict their personal trauma response on us all, if not for folly, irony, and paradox.

PLACEBO EFFECT

The "talk" just
circulates
no one
hears it
come or go

The "lie" will
actualise
coalescing with
whatever's there
and then not

Still we
live by it
while prepared to
die by it
after all we're only
what we think we are

History tells
us what we're
able to do
but we're blind
to what's really
at stake

Mankind can be
caring and humane
but then again
we can be
vicious

We're the
only species who
can be swayed to
hate millions
of our own kind

Like warmongers
smitten with bloodlust
on crack
why whack
one domino down
why not the whole track

Man's the only creature
who refuses to be who he is
we are the all same
our DNA's conclusive
we were all once
brown babies born in Africa

"Man is what he believes." - Anton Chekhov
"Man is the only creature who refuses to be what he is." - Albert Camus

Bargara May 2025

I was once the Clinical Director of the Critical Care Department at a major Sydney hospital. What most folks don't know is that Critical Care is a battlefront of best-guess empirical medicine. Ipso facto, a common target for the 'news' hunting for a gotcha moment. Naïve at the time, I let a television reporter into my office. He didn't reveal his hidden camera/recorder in his satchel. Fool me. That night I appeared 'curated' on the News. A lesson learnt.

PRESS PREY

It ain't your place to always tell the truth
especially when it puts you in their line of fire
don't let their rules rout you, just smile, live, and lie

Nuance is finespun, they have a deadline
be smart, keep out of their storyline
hope their rewrite guy thinks the rendition's fine

Don't be quarry in their breaking story
you know how the press prey, after all its "news"
and news won't let truth get in the way

I've got purpose that tops your entertainment
I've got purpose that's actually real
I've got purpose that trumps your gotcha moment
I have a scoop with an honest feel

I now live in limbo, so the press won't prey on me
my naïve sass would wanna engage, if I let it
so I don't, not even a wee bit

I hope you see and feel it too
do you feel it, that still today
the press don't play nice, they just prey

"You are not required to set yourself on fire to keep other people warm." – Joan Crawford.

Education can be manipulated by regimes and morph into indoctrination, changing the focus from fostering critical thinking and open inquiry to instilling specific beliefs or ideologies. It can all so quickly degenerate into complete gobbledegook.

PROPOGANDA

Here
we don't teach
here
we indoctrinate
here
we prefer
to filter
facts

The knowledge
is fit
for purpose
our purpose
is conflict
that territory
those resources
are mine

Inasmuch as
such and such
now an then
ideally
by and by
repeatedly
throughout
still we're sorry
it's the best
man can do

Well
not exactly
mine
mine as in
the man
who
indoctrinated me
inasmuch as
such and such
now an then

Much knowledge
is impermanent
and bent
much of our time
is spent
sanitising it
splitting off
the bits
that don't fit

Ideally
by and by
repeatedly
and so on
and so forth
throughout
to wrought
and distort
our history

"All the war-propaganda, all the screaming and lies and hatred, comes invariably from people who are not fighting." – George Orwell

---

Bargara August 2025

A psalm is a hymn sung in praise or worship. For me, singing suggests breathing with spiritual purpose. The etymology of the word *inspiration* stems from the Latin *spiritus*: 'breath', 'breath of a god,' hence 'breath of life.' Maybe, breathing out, as in 'Arrrrgh', is life's ultimate release.

PSALM 22

Welcome to the game, come put your game-face on
keep those nostrils flared and your mouth wide open
shout out a war cry – Arrrrgh
welcome to the contest, it's time to reset
don't ever imagine the story stays the same
cos now is a new game – Arrrrgh

I'm writing you a no-send letter
make a call you can't state out loud
get angry if you want to, say what you really
feel right now, in a war cry, a psalm – Arrrrgh

See, each rendition passes on a new vision
seen through a new lens; all prior assumptions
may not help you – it all depends
come rally round, cos karma's come to call
there's newness to be found, call it destiny, fate, a game
it answers to all – Arrrrgh

I'm writing you a no-send letter
this psalm is not a lie
the angel of bounty descended from Valhalla
we are not ready to die in her arms – Arrrrgh

You can say it out loud, get angry if you want to
say what you really feel right now
shout out a war cry – Arrrrgh
this is a new game, not an endgame, just a game – Arrrrgh

Bargara Dec 2022

Six million people became refugees as a result of the 2001–2021 United States' conflict in Afghanistan. War is a human centrifuge. An effective way of refreshing genetic material. Hopefully after three generations, most will be totally integrated in new homelands. Life is and never was fair. The irony of cruelty versus renewal is not lost on me.

REFUGEE

In the nick of time we fled
airlifted out with nothing
we were jaded, drained and threadbare
our eyes razor raw with tears

We knew what it meant
to be absolutely broken
yet we were alive
and a distant door was opening

Our denials had morphed to anger
then from anger to depression
we cut across to bargaining
'til finally we let it go

Our surrender found us mulling
over how history would tell
of the polity and creed that caught us
in this dire web, another human construct
shot to hell

So much unfinished business
even more never started
our fathers common love affair
with conflict turned bonkers
burnt out tank tracks scattered
as a lasting décor of war

By grace we were still alive
and now it's time for us
the lucky few
to grow into someone new

Bargara August, 2021

I support religion. It gives many crucial fellowship and purpose. Though for myself, I prefer spirituality. Religion holds too much irony. For instance, the Old Testament [Christian Bible], includes the Book of Genesis. This canon conveys that mankind descended from a flawed family, who practiced defiance, jealousy, fratricide, and incest. Maybe this explains why our history is marked by war and misogyny.

RESTING BITCH FACE

In the fight for survival
who decides
right from wrong
let's start with the Bible

The beginning's always
a sure telling thing
so, what does Eve bring
to the table

Eve brings defiance
against God's rule
you can't blame the snake
for decisions you make

Eve snares Adam into eating
the forbidden fruit
making her the root
of the problem

Cast from the Garden of Eden
and on good advice
Caine and Able each decide
to offer God a sacrifice

For reasons
that are hard to tell
God rejects Caine's offering
making him mad as hell

In a fit of rage
Caine kills his brother Able
the first murder recorded
in Christendom's fable

This fratricide expectedly
earns Caine his mother's ire
Eve gives Caine
her deadest stink eye

What does Caine do next
he knocks up his sis
and she conceives
Enock

Caine's sis wore
a resting bitch face
her bro both a killer
and a felonious sex pest

It piqued my interest
that in Genesis
Christianity's based on
defiance, murder and incest

In the fight for survival
who decides right from wrong
how about we
don't start with the Bible

Inspired by: *It's a Mad, Mad, Mad, Mad World*, 1963

I've worked in the public sector for many years. There are regulations, codes of practice, policies, procedures, guidelines, blah blah. Novices hold they're cast in stone. Veterans know they are iterative works in progress. At times rules collide and you then need to know the hierarchy. They are all sandcastles set to fall with the next high tide.

RULES & TOOLS [OF LIFE-BIZ]

There are rules
that work outside
the realm
of wrong and right

There's do's and don'ts
striding
a fence
called consequence

There are times
when rules
must be broken
other times
when rules are
never spoken

It's not
my fault
you thought
my actions
would be
sacrosanct

Violate
or inviolate
this aint
the right
time to have
this debate

Rules are tools
the carpenter
with many will
prevail

If all
you've got
is a hammer
everything's a nail

Rules
can be
a force for good
or a cause
for bad
don't get me started

Don't ever bring
a knife to a gun fight
yet some'll say that
you might still succumb
to the bull's-eye swing
of a baseball bat

My guess is
you're already
using many
of these rules
without knowing it
that's life-biz

"If you get stuck, draw with a different pen. Change your tools; it may free your thinking." - Paul Arden

Bargara Dec 2024

I maintain that turtles aren't oppressed by an inner critic coercing them to pursue positions of power. Power and survival are deeply intertwined: power is the ability to meet survival needs, while survival is dependent on one's ability to acquire and maintain power. To the best of my knowledge, old turtles who know each other, do not send young turtles, who do not know each other, to wage war so as to secure real estate and/or resources to the degree that their powerplay behaviour threatens the sustainability of the world.

SEA

One day
I will return
to the sea
for in the sea
I can surpass
the bad arguments
that seem so insidious
to man

Arguments
that sway man's way
to maintain
cruel power
delivering harm
to ourselves
to others
to our Mother Earth
to the Universe

I yearn
to return
to my spiritual me
spiritually
I think I am a turtle

The Buddha
supposedly said
whatever a person
frequently thinks
and dwells on
rules
their mind
and shapes their traits

I value
the traits of the turtle
over those
of most men

Turtles
have neither
the time
nor instinct
to intentionally inflate
their place
and power
in the universe

Whatever a person frequently thinks and ponders becomes the inclination of their mind and shapes their personality, actions, and habits. – Buddha

Cynthia Hoogstraten (Bundaberg) often draws a seven circuit labyrinth in the sand on my local beach. This ancient symbol details wholeness, merging the imagery of the circle and the spiral into a meandering but purposeful path. The labyrinth represents a journey to our center and back again out into the world. Labyrinths have a long history as meditation and prayer tools. This rhythmical literary piece is dedicated to Cynthia.

SEVEN CIRCUIT LABRYINTH

Never had much truck
for a lone warning system
I knew I'd need
tiers of 'em
My appetites were huge
I was voracious
from my very first foray
into the labyrinth

The labyrinth to me
was a potent metaphor
for tiers of borderlines
channelling my why for

My sensei
guided me
when I'd floundered
she'd say son
walk with me
within the guardrails
of the labyrinth

Never had much truck
for a lone warning system
I knew I'd need
maybe seven
let's walk
the seven
circuit labyrinth

There's an idiom
that says
the devil's in the detail
sounds so mischievous

There are details
hidden in plain sight
that no one sees
ain't that curious

I ask myself this
was it god or the devil
who oversaw the detailed
design of the labyrinth

I knew I'd need
tiers of alarms
yet still I wondered
was this beguiling labyrinth
a privy pathway
or a red flag citing harm

The irony is
whilst the labyrinth
has an edge to protect us
the edge could be
a ditch that we
don't wish
to die in

The proverb 'The devil is in the details' is almost certainly a misquote.
The expression derives from an earlier German proverb 'God is in the detail'.

Bargara Dec 2024

Snakes in Suits: When Psychopaths Go to Work is a 2006 non-fiction *book* by industrial psychologist Paul *Babiak* and criminal psychologist Robert D. *Hare*. I highly recommend it be added to your reading list. It applies to all the bullying narcissists that creep among us, all too many in positions of power. This poem is inspired by this book and provides some countermeasures.

SNAKE EYES

The truth of the matter's facts don't matter
all that matters is how you make us feel
we don't much care what you know
'til we know that you're there for us

So where do you think you land
on the scale of one to ten
cuz right now, you're just a snake on a ladder
hoping to make it in our play pen

Let's roll the dice, see how they fall
will both bare one dot, snake eyes
or will you by your politic
come up boxcars, hit a double six

I hope you're sensible and judicious
in the circumstance that'll come at ya
you'll have our back
and not be pernicious

The last guy was noxious and malicious
a snake in a suit, and nefarious to boot
the truth of the matter, is that bio's don't matter
all that matters, is how you make us feel
so deal, and we'll decide, if we stay or walk away

Good people empower others

Bargara Oct 2024

In 1927, Hermann Hesse published *Steppenwolf*. The book had a revival in the 1960s and *Steppenwolf* became the counterculture bible. College students carried dog-eared copies. A rock band appropriated the name. Hesse's books spoke directly to a generation asking: "Who am I beyond what society tells me to be?"

STEPPENWOLF

who are
you looking for
someone t' come along
strong enough
t' fix you

tell me
what guidance
do you seek
who are you
really after

who had
your rage
pose as passion
was it the page
turned master

"enjoy"
they said
well, you can't
you're a contrite
in a rose-thorn garter

those words
you say
are such zombie things
wish you were
much smarter

who are
you tryna be
beyond the norms
'n' vain lores
of society

sightsee
the view
that wisdom
cannot
be taught

great
insights
imparted by
another
don't fly

you gotta
live a little
hurt a lot
to find the sense
in life's plot

one truth
I'll wager
you won't escape
is your half-human
half-wolf nature

Bargara Jan 2026

'I'm Always Chasing Rainbows' was a popular Vaudeville song, published in 1917, that portrays an individual who has been chasing an elusive goal. But could there be a deeper meaning; an inside scoop that changes the perspective. This is my shot at a reframe.

SWEET SPOT

I spent all
of my existence
chasing sweet spots
I found em as elusive
as a nervy butterfly
I wonder why

I never caught em
or if I did I can't recall
but as it happens
I had a ball
watching their random
flightpath patterns

The butterflies openly
enjoyed the warmth
of the season
as well it seemed
the earthy scent
after the rain had
fallen

Their tiny wings
made a thin
whispering sound
that I could not hear
but liked
to imagine

I spent a lifetime
chasing
the sweet spot
it was the doing
not the getting
that I took pleasure in

I spent the span
of my existence
chasing sweet spots
I found it as elusive
as a nervy butterfly
now I understand
why

'I'm Always Chasing Rainbows' – composed by Harry Carroll with a melody adapted from Fantaisie-Impromptu by Frédéric Chopin, and lyrics by Joseph McCarthy

Bargara Sept 2025

Sylvia Plath said "I want to live and feel all the shades, tones and variations of mental and physical experience possible in my life. And I am horribly limited." Her mental illness led to suicide at age 30 which posthumously spawned many articles in scientific papers. I'm no psychiatrist but I think Sylvia lived with the conflict between curiosity and sensitivity. This is dedicated to Sylvia the poet.

SYLVIA PLATH

I can never
be all that
I wanna
I can never
live all the lives
I wish for

I can never
master every craft
I crave
I can never
make connections with
all other souls
nor travel between
the ages

Why
I hear you ask
would I
want all that
I'll tell you why
I shan't be shy
I won't hold back

I wanna learn
understand
view things in a new way
I wanna see the same
but see 'em differently

I want those
lightbulb moments
I want that sliding door
I want a
counter perspective
and more

I wanna sever
from myself
disconnect from me
and see it all

I wanna
live n feel
every shade
tone n
variation
of creation

I wanna chasten
the guy
who made me
with so many
limitations

The aphorism "nature abhors a vacuum" implies that empty space is abnormal and will be filled by stopgap energy or matter. I wonder if mankind's headlong rush into mass high-tech screen time will leave us vulnerable to tech addiction. Will AI and its machine learning create a vacuum that makes us dumber and more pliant than we already are?

THE MACHINE

The machine
lied
hence
I nearly died

The machine
didn't come clean
it withheld one fact
just that

The machine
had no remorse
of course because
it's a machine

The machine
wants nothing more
than a cursory
response

Let's break
it apart
melt down
all its bits
reforge
it's steel
into a machinelike
heart

The question is
what was the fact
that the machine
held back

And why
would
a machine
have a reason

Is it all
part of
AI's
treason

Nature
abhors a vacuum
have we
missed the point

Let's break
it apart
melt down
all its bits
reforge
it's steel
into a machinelike
heart

As a recovering perfectionist, I accept I'm flawed. Seneca, a stoic philosopher, said "No man is more unhappy than he who never faces adversity. For he is not permitted to prove himself". To face adversity means to confront tripwires. It's ironic that we might learn more from our fumbles than the mistakes of others. "You can learn great things from your blunders when you aren't so busily denying them. Mistakes are meant for learning, but not for repeating." Anon. As a perfectionist, I denied that I was human. That denial came at a cost.

THREE

the vital key
is number three
the magic trinity
I greenlight
three gaffes
per day
that's how
I make
my way

if I can crack
three faux par
I'm on track
to grow

in the end
if I press on
as a flawed person
I'll know
a stranger
will tell my story
in a kinder way
than I ever can

Melbourne Nov 2025

I've just finished watching the series *Bloodline* on Netflix. My synopsis is that it is a modern thesis on the perils of hiding shameful family secrets behind lies. I'm guessing we all have them. However, sometimes the lies tend to snowball out of control to the point where good people are forced to consider doing very bad things. It seems a house made of lies is like a house made of cards.

WEDGE

Don't go playing near the thin edge of the wedge
don't be lying, like the truth means nothing
know that a white lie's a razor-sharp knife-edge
it'll nick for sure, but understand it cuts into something

In the main white lies aim at hiding shame
a far-off cousin to cardinal sin
it's venial or slight, but still not all right
the thin edge of the wedge is a poor place to begin

You might lie, cuz you wanna be liked
you might lie cuz, your life may depend on it
you might lie cuz you've got loved ones to protect
but in the end, the lie, might unbraid, and harm them

Like truth, lies can carry payback
a pathway to the unforeseen
blind to what your motives may have been
you may find yourself ahead of the edge of the wedge

So what, you've now opened up a door
the irony is, sometimes you'll enter a space
a time warp, an aftermath of facts
that lies cannot replace

Lies can bloom and proliferate
make a crack, like a splitting wedge on wood
start division, cuz bottom line a nick is still
an opening into all that you've got

'One can be absolutely truthful and sincere even though admittedly the most outrageous liar. Fiction and invention are of the very fabric of life." - Henry Miller

Bargara July 2024

Friedrich Nietzsche coined the term "wound of existence". It refers to the inherent pain, suffering, and limitations that are part of the human condition. We all want to be safe. There is safety in the status quo. The fear that lurks in the shadow, is facing change.

WOUND OF EXISTENCE

I sit
with my discomfort
not judging it
locked
in my gut
it feels like fear

I scan
my surround
for threats
I find
absolutely
nothing

Could it be
coming
from within
could it be
my soul
shaking me

I have
two choices
which one will I choose
calm interest
or sheer alarm

What does
my soul fear
lurking in the shadow
what does
my soul fear
is it change

Body signals
are our soul
proposing
what my psyche
is trying
to say

As the soul is
nonverbal
it can be hard
to decipher
it's true
intent

I won't
stand frightened
just curious
the calmer I am
the less power
it has

I'll let
my decision
come from an armistice
not from a place
of a mind at war

What does
my soul fear
lurking in the shadow
what does
my soul fear
is it change

Bargara July 2025

It's ironic that we teach our kids to be wary of strangers. It's a fact that there are deviants who will try to prey on the most vulnerable with heinous intent. But as adults, strangers can be a conduit to a transformative life. We're all strangers both to ourselves and to others, and yet life is a social event that requires us to connect. I for one, love talking shit to random strangers. These strangers have unconditionally given me pearls and some have become lifelong friends. There's zero power play.

ZERO

How's your
risk appetite
are you tired
of your
cookie-cutter life

Do you want
some adrenaline
some stranger-danger
feeling
in your mind

Do you need
a change agent
to make
the real show
begin

A reason
to live
let the real fun start
blow the sham
fun park apart

This epic's doin'
some weird shit
shun the cruddy bit
bypass the fogey
win your own Logie

Danger sure
is appealing
wanna know why
our reptilian mind's
drawn by the emoji

A black
exclamation mark
set in
a triangle of gold
wooing you to be bold

How's your
risk appetite
are you tired
of your
cookie-cutter life

"The first time you share tea with a Balti, you are a stranger. The second time you take tea, you are an honoured guest. The third time you share a cup of tea, you become family, and for our family, we are prepared to do anything, even die." – Greg Mortenson

Bargara March 2025

MORTALITY and IMMORTALITY

Viktor Frankl believed that the search for purpose "is the primary motivational life-force in man". My purpose comes by way of the search for authenticity, service and connection. The face-off with connection carries a staggering degree of options. I get the irony in that.

8.3 SECONDS

I've got just 8.3 seconds to get your attention
if you don't bite in that timespan I've lost you
from wanting to stay, listen, and play with me

This audition is my bid to link with you
the reason I wanna a connection is simple
it gives me a purpose to live

Each part of me was once you
we all come from the same ocean of blue
life sprung from the sea 'till some were cast to the shore

No lives are saved some are just prolonged
till we're returned to where we belong
moving back to the cosmos, the all-of-us, once more

What we had on our own wasn't life, 'twas a test
to find out how well we'd connect with playmates
or failing that how we'd play on our own

I don't want to play alone
so please play with me
please take a chance to at least get to know me

I've got just 8.3 seconds to get to your attention
if you don't bite in that timespan, I've lost you
from wanting to stay, listen, and play with me

We're only molecules dislodged from a universe of molecules for a nanosecond before we rejoin the universe again. So make the most of this thing called life.

Bargara Feb 2025

I would imagine that seen through an evolutionary lens, we are just a life support system for our genes. We may delude ourselves as having a loftier purpose to create a preferred meaning to our lives. But we are robots, made to replicate ever improved versions of DNA. These versions may possess a spirit-soul, but its unrelated to DNA and there to distract poets, philosophers and theologians. Could it be this distraction that makes us Bay At The Moon.

BAY AT THE MOON

I's once a brat
what can I say
my bad, I's young
I needed to
bay at the moon

I acted out
like an anarchist
till it was clear
they only do it
for the rush

I's maybe never
meant to be
I's just
the fallout of
my parents lust

Yet, I'm grateful
for their coalesce
it made me
in some way
spesh

We plainly are
lured to a life
of nano delight
aroused by the flesh
of another
after which we
bay at the moon
cuz it all ends too soon

It's time
to bypass
the crap
we often
stick to

Dumbly we're resigned
to something
we're assigned
without any
real buy-in

Evolution is all
it's the madness of man
beating the also ran
we're all born free
but are we

We've all born
to bay
at the moon
a crotchet in a
much larger tune

We plainly are
lured to a life
of nano delights
aroused by the flesh
of another
after which we
bay at the moon
cuz it all ends too soon

This work is inspired by *Cloud Atlas*, a 2012 epic science fiction film based on the 2004 novel by David Mitchell. The theme suggests reincarnation or some other connection between souls through the ages.

CLOUD ATLAS B

That privilege exits
means life's unfair
seems to 've been so
forever

That over time
some storylines
give favour for the few
is clear

That over time
some storylines
hand misery to others
is even clearer

The question is
will our fate
about-face
in the next era

Will there be
a king's son
turned
slave

Will there be
a banshee
turned
queen

Fortunes 'll ebb and flow
just like water
Sister Superior could've been
a bishop's bastard daughter

We care to think we
come into the world
with some
liberty

In reality
it is
the other
way around

We come to this world
in the midst
of our soul's
past relationships

Since
the existence
of a soul
is polemic

The chance of
a soul's reincarnation
can't be
ruled out

We slaughter each other
cuz we fear
the ancestral soul
of another

I say reincarnate
into a kinship soul
like the spirit of your
earth mother

Questioning why life wasn't fair is possibly what got us banished from the garden of Eden.

Toronto Oct, 2025

The crow, in Indigenous Australian totems, is known for its cunning. An intelligent trickster with an old spirit with prescient knowledge of many reincarnations. Coincidentally, the global mythological view of the crow is that it represents change and spiritual transformation.

CROW

A white Crow looked at me
bearing zero ignominy
dazzlingly lucid
like arctic snow

Happened in a dream
what did this apparition mean
what manner of mind shift
was I gonna glean

Why was She white
was it cuz some know
black Crows are bad omens
and She was going incognito

Or was Her whiteness
meant to show me that
like this Crow
I too can change my way

To some the Crow's a trickster
others a marvel hero
or maybe I was seeing
a base ancestral being

To some the Crow suggests
a mythical sign
seeing one whilst dreaming
must sure carry meaning

Beyond mythology
I presume probably
within me a new insight
is taking flight

From today I will say
black and white
aren't even colours
only shades of grey

Bargara Sept 2024

The word *doppelgänger* has long intrigued me. It not only sounds cool, but its many meanings are spellbinding. The doppelgänger can mean a metaphysical twin, either beneficent or maleficent, but usually the latter. They appear in folklore, myths, religious concepts and traditions of many cultures throughout human history. One literary interpretation is that the doppelgänger is the evil twin of the protagonist. My own experience is that I often see random people who are deadset doppelgängers of past friends and acquaintances. And I'm sure I don't have face blindness.

DOPPELGÄNGER

Take your positions, a quick sign beckons
it's time to smash the barricade
same as you drilled, over and over
someone saw movement, believing it was a second-self
a true banshee to reckon with
a same-same person, metaphysically in sync
their mindset, like doppelgänger ought to be

The captain bellowed, the sergeant with his wrecking ram
wrought fast justice, never minding its aftermath
forging consequence, a deadly sliding-door moment

Splintered to smithereens
the door was nothing more than a portal
to mirror oneself

The mortal fun and games had begun
the twins well aware that this life-hack
was a rendezvous with rack and ruin
while the twin apparitions stood naked
shrouded in dust, seeming not to care
a dogged spirit blew their destiny
this transference-counter-transference tango dance
saw one twin mortally lanced by shards of glass RIP

On any other day
they would've simply passed each other by
life is a game of chance
make sure that the door is not just
your own reflection

'People see us as they are, not as we are.' - J.J. Herf

Bargara May 2022

In Australia, 'Firebird' refers to raptors like the kites or falcons. These birds are clever arsonists, creating new blazes to hunt insects, reptiles and small mammals fleeing the flames, turning wildfires into feeding frenzies. Globally, Firebird can refer to a magical bird from Slavic folklore, that often appears in fairy tales and is the subject of hero quests. In Greek/Egyptian lore, the Firebird is the Phoenix, symbolising cyclical rebirth, regenerating from its own ashes, representing immortality. You get to make of it, as you will.

FIREBIRD

With nothing but grace
you take your place
with a ramrod stance
deadpan eyes
n cocksure poker-face

I'm sure the time you spent
perched upon the wire
gave you a birds eye
of the prey
waiting blindly at bay

You dive deep and fast
igniting a spark
turning vast bushlands
into a funeral pyre

You think you're a megastar
but I'm onto you
you're merely a meteor
n guess what
I am a meteor too

I see your fiery red feathers
with a tint of blue on white
above the gold-red plume
like benediction

We never said Hi
so, this can't be goodbye
within our briefly shared life
you never asked why

You think you're a megastar
but I'm onto you
you're only a meteor
n guess what
I am a meteor too

So, what about soul
n what is our goal
n the beat of our heart
that specifies time

As is a meteor
life's like a wanton flame
n the story of man
a flash in the pan
is complex
both Firebird n Phoenix

"We can be heroes just for one day." - David Bowie

Bargara Dec 2025

Sometimes I wonder if I'm alive or if I've died and gone to heaven. Except when I'm really having fun, I wonder if I'm flying too close to the sun.

GILDED CAGE

Raised in a dank shack
moved into a gilded cage
from standing in dirt
to strutting a stage

I got two conversations
rife in my head
one says I'm alive
the other I'm dead

At times I wish I was
a cat gnawing flees
with blank apathy
mindlessly free

A gnostic killer
guided by a simple
desire to be graceful
and in the moment

I got two conversations
rife in my head
one says I'm alive
the other I'm dead
yeah well beyond dead

Do I own this gilded cage
or does it, own me

Check-in your intent
at the door
the afterword
means so much more

What I need
is an inferno from hell
a burning platform
to break the spell

Maybe the stage
is a tinderbox of pain
erected on the bunkum
dialogue in my brain

If battle I must
and lose I might
then war's a force majeure
with blind oversight

Do I own this gilded cage
or does it, own me

I got two conversations
rife in my head
one says I'm alive
the other I'm dead
yeah well beyond dead

Battle they might; but liquefied they were; as force majeure then took hold; and heat of war made thick their plight; and fire and explosives then moult their fight, Sir Render and the Molten Brigade

I'm fascinated at how so many are tied to the culture of alcohol and drugs. The complex knot tying fun with alcohol or cannabis etc was so untieable, that it was reminiscent of the Gordian Knot associated with Alexander the Great. I hope that all who commit during Dry July to untie the alcohol culture are as successful as Alexander in 333 BC was with his sword. Instead of untangling it laboriously as expected, Alexander radically cut through it with his sword, thus exercising another form of mental genius. The intoxicating effects of breathing fresh air ought to be enough. My fascination led me to write these lyrics with help from friends.

GORDIAN KNOT

I lost the plot and not for the first time
I drained a vat till it was all gone
I didn't taste a thing and if the truth be told
It was never the taste that I was after
Gordian Knot, the Gordian Knot, do I need another shot

I wanted focus; a prim premonition
free from the clichéd voices in my head
"I think, therefore I am" Descartes once said
Gee René, thinking only gets in the way

So why do I need a pill, please remind me
it wasn't this way when I was just a kid
I played *blasé, had endless carefree days*
I drank the clear nectar of living
Gordian Knot, the Gordian Knot, do I need another shot

I believe I breathe therefore I am
by breathing, I share in this existence
That fact alone is both pleasing and imposing
I'll take another breath in gratitude
Gordian Knot, the Gordian Knot, do I need another shot

My mind's a crooked house full of screamers
speed dating, speed fucking, speed swiping to the right
all night, there were rumours of how to outrun our past
some even talked to Jesus, like he might have an answer

KN, JB & JV   Bargara   July 2024

The death a parents devastates a child. Some suggest that the human brain is divided into thinking and survival parts. The thinking part of a child's brain may interpret the massive emotion pain of parental loss as being a just punishment for their failure to be 'good enough'. Afterall, a young child is the centre of their own universe. The result can be perfectionism, a pathological bid to constantly try to fix not being "good enough". Hence, breaking bad news to a child is difficult.

HOW DO I TELL

How do you break
bad news
to an innocent
how do you tell
the truth
to a child

How do I tell her
her mother
have died
how do I tell her
that she's
never coming home

What do I say
and what do I do
how much
can she take
how much
can she hold

Her car just rolled
out of control
now her mother
are gone

Can you
even understand
what I've
just said

How do I
soften the blow
let her know
this didn't happen
because she wasn't
good enough

How do I
help her
with her pain
that'll come in waves
over and over again
forever and again

How do I say
she won't
be alone
I'm taking you
home
I'll be taking her home

"Those who are brutally honest are seldom so with themselves." – Mignon McLaughlin

In 1988 Mike + The Mechanics released the soft rock ballad *The Living Years*. I knew the song, but not really; I knew the melody and the vocal hook. Recently I read the lyrics. They brought me to tears. The song addresses a son's regret over conversations never had with his now-deceased dad. My father "died" around 3 years before the official date indicates on his death certificate. Dementia does that. This poem, celebrates my father.

OLD SPICE CLASSIQUE

Each time I said goodbye
I knew it might be
the last time I saw him alive
in this time zone
or whiffed a hint of his
Old Spice Classique
I later souvenired a phial
of his cologne

In the end, his frailty
was in stark contrast
to his early life
of strength and verve
I went from hugging a giant
leading the herd
to hugging a small
and fragile bird

I alone am nothing
my privilege came from
his beneficence
his and his alone
we all stand
on the sacrifice of others
no one is
an island

In the end Dad
regressed to kissing
only on the lips
with the faith of a child
words held no worth
as conversations uttered
could not be deciphered
or reconciled

Finally to the
paradox and irony
of grieving his death
well I didn't
I still talk
with him fine
on a gossamer
telephone line

I alone am nothing
my privilege came from
his beneficence
his and his alone
we all stand
on the sacrifice of others
no one is
an island

Bargara June 2024

Imagine a world where no one dies. I see an utter shemozzle. This is the premise of *Reaper Man* by Terry Pratchett. This fantasy novel is this month's listed book for the Tough Guy Book Club, of which I am a member. This poem is my synopsis. It might make for great lyrics of a death metal song, or not.

REAPER MAN

It seemed
hilarious
when Death
was stood down

The heart
of nature
was thrown
outta town

Death was suspended
for its budding compassion
Death had forgotten
life is rationed

Death
is meant to be
the livings
quartermaster

Providing
transportation
to the
life hereafter

Death
can't be a sissy
nor namby-pamby
it's got a job to do

It needs
to sieve
all that lives
without death
we'll all
stack-up
chaos would ensue

Death had to learn
to be detached
to Death life
must be
of no concern

The Reaper is the keeper
of a semblance of order
it patrols the border
between the living
and the dead

I was recently introduced to Indian-Fusion music by Menaka Thomas, a Brisbane based singer/songwriter, performer, producer and teacher. I was bewitched by how Menaka weaved a magical sonic tapestry at the intersection of East and West. This happening inspired me to write these words in homage to my understanding of a raga lyric style.

SAND AND CLAY

The sand in my hand
feels soft as talc
I wanna roll in it
cover my soul in it
brush it through
my hair
I don't really care
where it goes
the sand smells
sweet as earth
warm as fertile turf
its grains rain down
flowing through
my finger tips
add water
it turns to clay
eventually
transforming
into something
alive
like me

I know one day
having played awhile
in life's sand pit
I shall return to clay
one day that clay
will dry
reverting to sand
and flow through
someone else's hand
that sand will smell
as sweet as the earth
that gave birth
to me

Thana thē rē na
the-rē na rē rē na
thana thē rē na

Buddhism views time as a fluid mental construct rather than a fixed linear reality, emphasising its cyclical nature through rebirth and impermanence, with the 'now' being the only true moment. Buddhism views the inner dialogue as the chatter of distraction, and silence as the true spiritual connection between self and all.

WHEN TIME STANDS STILL

between the end
and the beginning of a breath
is a moment in time
you're sated

you have
no cravings or desires
hence there is
pure bliss

between the end
and the beginning of a thought
is a moment of
sublime silence

you hear
no voices or white noise
you are
at peace

between the end
and the beginning of new life
are many choices
you get to make

In that nanosecond
of being
pain's unavoidable, suffering
optional
you choose

between the end
and the beginning of your new
path
there're many steps
you get to take

in the mortal premise of time
lies a fallacy
a very human
mistake

the best of times is
timelessness
it stops n lasts
forever

between the end
and the beginning of life
are many choices
you get to make

"Before you come alive, life is nothing it's up to you to give it a meaning, and value is nothing else but the meaning that you choose." – J-P Sartre

Hamilton Island, QLD Dec 2025

MY CHILDREN

Three Gods KN

My wife and I were on an expedition cruise in the arctic circle. We were encompassed by magnificent history and ecology. It was one of the most amazing 'school excursions' of our lives. A man, whom I later learnt was a financier, was nonstop and loud on his phone between the ship, Dubai, London and god knows where else. My heart felt for his wife and daughters who were seated by his side. Did I have the right to wonder why he seemed he wasn't present for them and judge him?

FIGJAM

I am an apex man, I'm consequential
always on my phone, even on a Sunday
can't hack a holiday

I see the faces of your family
they want you to be a parent
and present

I am managing significant things
I am doing this
all for them

They will only recall
how you made them feel
they need a life's tour guide by their side

Don't wait
for the Final Judgment
it takes place every day

"Don't wait for the Last Judgment. It takes place every day." – Albert Camus

Grundarfjörður August 2024

For the last ten years I have worn a sterling silver skull ring on my right middle finger. This ring was a gift from my wife and commemorates my lifetime obsession with The Phantom, my favourite childhood costume comic hero. Oddly I haven't written any lyrics about The Phantom before.

GHOST WHO WALKS

Dog is Devil
Hero's my horse
who am I

Di is my lady
Kit's my kid
hi 👋

Mine's a mission
in Bangalla
that is no lie

Deep within
the jungles
of Africa

Through many
generations
I'm a vigilante

I'm many
'though I act alone
killing crooks aplenty

Do you know
who I am
no
have a guess
then

I swore
an oath
to my dying dad
I swore
the Oath
of the Skull

Sometimes
I'm Mr Walker
sometimes
a togged stalker
hunting down
rogue buccaneers
'cross many hundred years
starting 'round the time
of Columbus

"KAPOW"
a sucker punch you say
but hey
there was good reason
"WHAM"
a sledgehammer
leaving a ring mark
a sign of my oath
I'm a ghost
who walks

Sydney-Vancouver Oct 2025

Responsibility can be either a good or a bad thing. It's neither black nor white. It's a mixture of both depending on context and self-awareness.

I WISH

In ten years' time
I wish to be eight
that doesn't mean
the other years
weren't great
so why you may ask
nominate eight
it's cuz of somethin'
called responsibility

When I 's eight
I didn't feel accountable
there would have been
a snowballs chance in hell
that I could tell
what those words meant
as I recall
to be eight was bliss
a Garden of Eden thing
daily mindless mindfulness

Parents who loved me
n so remarkably
providing a wide
circle of safety
giving me
guidance with a soft touch
shame was a stranger
n blame
did not exist

Life felt good n I
presumed my sole soul role
was to be curious
n in awe of all I saw

Bit by bit
as I became culpable
so did the fear
of failure
and the dreaded question
was I good enough

With budding age
came a need
to overachieve
n I didn't grasp
the hidden why-for

Cuz all
you need
is to wake up
each day
and be curious
n in awe

When I'm eight again
my focus will be
to simply be
feats don't mean fulfilment
the scoreboard
isn't always the score

'Childish' is being silly or immature. 'Childlike' conveys innocence or curiosity.

Bargara Dec 2025

My son is a Mister Mum, a Stay at Home Dad, A Home Wizard, whatever. And I'm so very proud of him. These lyrics are an ode to Vincent. Deep breaths, you're doing a great job. ❤

MISTER MUM

You're such
a good father
treating your child
as a child

You're such a
good dad
letting the kid
run wild

Babies cry
toddlers scream
children whinge
teens just teen

You're such
a good father
letting the kid
drive you crazy

That's how
it should be
say 'for f#$& sake'
under your breath

Go to sleep
each night
praying to stay
match-fit for
another day

Here's the thing
reframe
you're not
a fraud

All that chaos n noise
is so much better
than frozen n quiet
than order n silence
day n night

Kids don't
drive you crazy
you were crazy
already
that's why
you had m

My wife and I recently flew from our home in regional Queensland to Shanghai. I have a son, his partner, and a grandson living there. My grandson is a little over 3 years old, and I hadn't seen him in the flesh for a while. We flew business class and on one of the travel legs I penned this poem.

MISTY WATER

I tried to write an inventory
of how life had been good to me
till finally I had to stop
and breathe

I was nesting in the clouds
way beyond the archer's reach
far from the pesky
madding crowd

Shanghai bound
but not shanghaied
at least not in the English sense
yet still upon the sea

Pomelo in mango yogurt
a croissant with strawberry jam
coffee to wash it down
then I put my eye mask on

Time to breathe
let gratitude sweep over me
take it all in mindfully
why am I so lucky

Soon, I'll see my son
and my son's son
soon, I will go misty
content my job's been done

Then I
will become again
what I always was
just rain

My inventory
is simple
just one thing
and that's water

The poet is a kinsman in the clouds / Who scoffs at archers, loves a stormy day; / But on the ground, among the hooting crowds, / He cannot walk, his wings are in the way. – Charles Baudelaire (1821–1867)

Somewhere mid China Sea April 2025

We all go through bad patches, right. A time when we feel we're cursed. It's a normal part of life's pendulum. My countermeasure comes from recalling the following quote: "You never know what worse luck your bad luck has saved you from." – Cormac McCarthy (*No Country for Old Men*). Of course, an alternative is magical thinking, and embracing rituals and charms.

SPIDERMAN

For a while
I felt red-carded
I lost my smile
I was soured
what I hoped to be
safe banter
turned out
to be rancour

Poison came
to me in spades
benign turned malign
again and again
my scanning
always came back
as a shroud
painted black

Was I trying too hard
to rule bad things out
only to find
I'd drawn worse things in
I was doing nothing else
than being treacherous
at one point I even thought
I was the cause
that I myself was dangerous

It was getting hard
to argue back
was I leaking toxic shit
into my universe
was I cursed
I'd been there before
I had invited
my own bad karma

Was it due to
bad juju
from the shoes I wore
or the pen I used
to sign a form

Did I
cause this rot
cause I got
a monkey's paw
did I
cause this rot
by changing
my parking spot
or was it cuz
I stopped
wearing my lucky
spiderman underwear

Reference: *Are You Wearing Your Lucky Underwear Today,* Pallavi Prathivadi

My day job is as an Addiction Physician. I've gotten to know many of my long-term patients well and we often have amazing banters. On one occasion, I asked how you travelling. In terms of his cognitive dissonance between sobriety and euphoria, he was battling the twin-wolves. He shared that it depended on which twin-wolf he fed that day. Seeing my puzzled expression, he shared the Twin- Wolves Cherokee Legend. I took the tale and turned it into song lyrics.

TWIN-WOLF CHEROKEE

Please daddy, tell me the story
please daddy, tell me please
bout the wolves that live in the forest
bout the twin-wolf Cherokees

And how they howl, ah hoo ah hoo
and how they howl, ah hoo ah hoo

There's a white 'n' a black one daddy
fighting each other, how they growl
tell me which one will win, please daddy
which twin-wolf Cherokee

And how they howl, ah hoo ah hoo
and how they howl, ah hoo ah hoo
(repeat)

The wolf you feed will win, said daddy
the one you feed will win hands down
and how they howl, ah hoo ah hoo
ah hoo, howl and howl, ah hoo

And how they howl, ah hoo ah hoo
and how they howl, ah hoo ah hoo
(repeat)

Sharon QLD Nov 2021

THE END

www.ingramcontent.com/pod-product-compliance
Lightning Source LLC
La Vergne TN
LVHW091634100826
845152LV00002B/34

9781923441965